ALISON
WONDERLAND

ALISON
WONDERLAND

A NOVEL

Helen Smith

MARINER BOOKS
HOUGHTON MIFFLIN HARCOURT
Boston   New York

First Mariner Books edition 2012

First published in 2011 by AmazonEncore

Library of Congress Cataloging-in-Publication Data is available

ISBN 978-0-547-84803-7

Printed in the United States of America
DOC 10 9 8 7 6 5 4 3

This book is for Lauren

1

The Crayfish

MY NAME'S ALISON TEMPLE and I used to have this line when people asked me if I'm married. I'd say, 'I'm waiting for Mr. Wonderland and when I find him I'll get married. Until then I'm staying single.' The kind of people who need to know whether or not you're married don't see the humour in a joke like that.

I was married once, for a while. I thought my husband was cheating on me. Sometimes he was late home and I'd stand at the bedroom window and watch the street. I'd lean against the window frame and press my forehead against the window in despair and I'd wonder, *Who do you love more than me?* In darkness, in silence, I'd wait until I saw him turn the corner on his way home. Then I'd go and lie in bed—waxwork, expressionless features; heavy, bloodless limbs. It was like one of those hospital nightmares where you have enough anaesthetic to stop you moving or screaming, but not enough to stop you feeling pain. I would just lie there, closing my eyes to stop the giddy feeling that I supposed was anger but was really relief that he was home at all. I was never sure which of us I hated more. Nothing tied me to him—not money, children, or even much of a shared history. Just a sunny day and a white dress. I stayed because I didn't want to leave, but I hated him for not loving me more than anyone else. I stood at the window and I wondered, *Who do you love more than me?* I never asked the question out loud.

I thought if I *knew* he was seeing someone else, then I'd have to leave. I wouldn't need to lie there anymore, waiting until he was asleep to touch his skin to see if it felt different, if someone else had touched it. I was twenty-four and I felt debilitated loving someone who didn't love me enough. I didn't want to leave him over a suspicion, but I didn't want to stay. I waited for a sign, something that would settle the matter for me.

One morning as I looked through a local paper while I was waiting for the kettle to boil to make myself a cup of coffee, I saw an advert for a female detective agency, and that's how I found this place: 'Fitzgerald's Bureau of Investigation. Discretion assured.'

I hired someone to follow my husband for two weeks, and I felt comfortable that a woman was doing it; I thought she'd understand. Was he unfaithful? I suppose I knew the answer in my heart a long time before it reached my head. I didn't hire the agency to prove that he was cheating; I wanted them to show me I was wrong. Yes, he was unfaithful.

The woman who had him followed was called Mrs. Fitzgerald. A tidy, authoritative woman in her late forties, she has slightly curling hair, cut severely short at the back in an old-fashioned crop. She calls her glasses spectacles. They're on a chain that she never puts round her neck. She waves them around or sets them down on the desk in front of her. Mrs. Fitzgerald has small, dainty feet and a large bosom and bottom. If you overheard a conversation about her in a butcher's shop, you'd catch a note of admiration when the men behind the counter called her a 'big woman.'

She handed me a colour photo that answered the question I'd never dared ask out loud.

'Do you really think he loves her more than me?' I peered at the photo in Mrs. Fitzgerald's office. From my experience of detective movies I'd expected it to be in black-and-white, but of course it's much cheaper and quicker to use colour film and get it developed in Boots.

'No, I don't suppose so, she looks rather bony and ordinary to me.'

That settled things for me. I just packed up and left him. I could have clung to him and wept, charmed him, fought with him, tried to hurt him or save him, if he'd been captivated by a bewitching, superior beauty. Perhaps the photo didn't do her justice, but I was rather disappointed in this thin girl he was fiddling about with in the evenings. Apart from a fleeting impulse—which I resisted—to call his girlfriend with some hair and makeup tips, I chose to ignore them both and faded spectacularly out of my husband's life.

That's not the whole story, of course. I wanted to get a can of red spray paint and write, 'You ruined my life, you bony bitch' all over the walls of her house and the place where she worked. I wanted to shred his clothes and castrate him. I wanted to call the police and get him into trouble. I mean, I really wanted someone to tell him off so he'd be sorry. I walked round and round town crying with shock and self-pity while I considered these options. In the end I compromised. I took half the money from our bank account, I bought a can of red spray paint and I went home. I packed everything I wanted from the house (not necessarily the things that were mine, just the things that I wanted, like his records), and then I put my wedding dress on the bed and I sprayed red paint on the bodice and I left a note by it: 'You broke my heart, you cunt.' He's never approved of women swearing. I didn't want him to feel sorry for me, I wanted him to be angry. *Then* I faded out of his life.

I work at the agency now. I've stopped waiting for Mr. Wonderland. I don't need him anymore.

One of my first jobs was for a woman who was worried that her husband was having an affair. They'd been married for years and they loved each other but they started having money troubles. He'd become withdrawn and secretive, going out in the evenings without telling her where he was going or who he was meeting. He'd come home late at night smelling of a brand of soap she didn't recognize. She thought he must be having sex with another woman and showering at her house before he came home.

I followed him to Clapham Common one night and tracked him as he sneaked through the men who gather there after nightfall in the hope of meeting a stranger, in spite of or perhaps because of the danger. They, like me, were warned as children never to talk to strange men, and now they want to meet them on the common and suck their cocks. They shot me furtive, guilty glances as I passed them, but I wouldn't meet their eyes in case they thought I was judging them.

I hung back in the trees as the unfaithful husband met a younger man he appeared to know. They greeted each other brusquely and moved away from the cruising area towards the pond. An island in the middle of the water is dedicated to the preservation of wildlife. There's a heron in Battersea Park, but the most exotic bird I've ever seen in Clapham Common is a Canada goose, which I believe is classified as a pest, along with grey squirrels.

The water is surrounded by concrete. There's a paved

lip from which parents with toddlers persevere in throwing stale bread, even though they must know it will choke and constipate any delicate-stomached ducks that might stop here en route to more glamorous locations. I'm not sure what the alternative is to feeding them bread. You're supposed to give hedgehogs dog food, but I can't see it working for wildfowl. Perhaps sunflower seeds, or perhaps, as the notice in the pond advises, you should leave them alone.

As far as romantic locations go, I've seen better. Swirls of greenish goose shit decorate the concrete surround of the pond. Ugly fish breed in the black water. Crayfish whose parents were plucked from a tank in an upmarket restaurant and released into a downmarket freedom here, where there is little else to do except feed and multiply, sit on the mud and open their mouths to let the plankton trickle in, oblivious to the sexual charge in the nearby cruising area.

The unfaithful husband and his boyfriend strode towards the ponds. Intrigued, I stood behind a tree and watched as they crouched at the water's edge. The foliage that hid me masked their activity but the urgency of their movements was unmistakable, so I moved closer. They were removing crayfish to return them to restaurants in the West End at market price. They worked quickly, stacking them in baskets in a dark blue van parked on the public road that runs through the Common along the edge of the pond. They need a permit to do this, and they didn't have one, which is why they met in secret. The husband washed the traces of pond and crustacea from his body at his friend's house before he went home to his wife so she wouldn't know the shameful things he'd been doing to make ends meet.

As I was new to the detective game I found the story

quite touching, and I didn't charge the wife for the time I spent following him, although she insisted I take the £7.99 it cost to get the photos developed. I still keep a picture of a crayfish in my wallet as a reminder that not everything is what it seems.

2

Taron & Jeff

THE DAY I get the call that changes my life is a Thursday. Four or five years have passed since I followed the man with the crayfish. I walk down to the office to pick up my cheque and catch up on my paperwork. It's April, the beginning of spring, with the watery sunshine and blue skies that make you look forward to summer. I'm not wearing a coat so I feel light and happy.

I pass our postman, who is psychic. He often comments on letters he's delivering. 'Good news,' he'll say, popping something through someone else's letterbox. I haven't had the opportunity to test whether his predictions are accurate, as he's never talked to me about my post. It's possible the only reason he knows it's good news is because he's delivering those letters from *Reader's Digest* which tell you on the outside of the envelope that you've won twenty-five thousand pounds. Even so, meeting him in the mornings always cheers me up. He ambles along, smoking a fag and stopping to talk to everyone he meets.

A postwoman in America was sacked recently for walking too slowly on her round. Her supervisor followed her and the letter of dismissal complained, 'Your lead foot was never more than one inch in front of the other.' Our postman doesn't even pick his feet up off the ground, so he'd never keep his job if he was working on the other side of the Atlantic. His uniform doesn't fit properly, or else he's customized it subtly, the way schoolchildren do, so that you know they're individuals underneath their regulation clothes. I wonder whether it's against the rules for him to smoke while on duty. It doesn't make much difference, as he's already in trouble for taking too much time off for the headaches caused by psychic phenomena. He has no post for me today as most of it goes to the agency these days, but he smiles as he passes me.

Ahead of me as I walk, a flash of sunlight on metal catches my eyes. An old woman is bending over a drain cover on the pavement, flipping coins through the grille and making wishes as the coins tumble towards the water below her.

The office is on the first floor of a red brick building, above a parade of shops. I cross over the road at the lights to get to it and look in through Woolworth's floor-to-ceiling plate glass windows as I walk past. I like the wide range of ordinary, comforting things they sell there: Pontefract cakes, coloured thread, gardening implements, Tupperware containers.

The call is from Taron, a dippy club chick I know vaguely who wants me to do some research. She used to run a club I went to sometimes in search of my lost youth after my marriage went down the pit. I gave her my phone number once when she admired the shoes I was wearing. It was an inappropriate response but the only one I could conjure at the time because the music was too loud to speak or think. Her saucer eyes were an indication that she was high and any attempt at conversation would be meaningless, anyway. She pointed with a finger tipped with pale tangerine varnish. 'Great shoes, where'd you get 'em?' and I, flattered by this endorsement from the Queen of Clubs, gave her a business card with my phone number (Alison Wonderland, I wrote on it) and my enigmatic ten-candle smile. One hundred candles glowed back.

I'm less surprised that she wants my help now than that she's managed to keep my number for so long.

'I need some information. Can you help me get it?'

'OK.' I'm opening my post but I have a pen and pad ready for the information she gives me over the phone.

'I need some statistics about which part of the country babies are abandoned most often, what time of year, and where to find them—outside hospitals or police stations or under hedges or in phone boxes.'

'Oh, OK. Yes, of course.' I crumple the envelopes and the flyers I've opened and shove them into the bin under my desk; then I move the phone receiver into my left hand and hold it against my left ear so that I can make some notes. *Mad cow*, I write.

I talk over her proposal with Mrs. Fitzgerald, who says I should take the case and charge twenty-five pounds per hour for the research. I like Mrs. Fitzgerald; I respect her. She has a reassuring presence. When I asked her for a job after I left my husband she told me to think it over for a few weeks.

'Take as long as you need to get things straight,' she said. 'Then if you're still interested, come and see me and I'll take you on as an investigator.' She spoke gravely, looking me carefully in the eyes to be sure I would understand that she was offering a professional opportunity.

'You've been to university,' she said. 'You could be valuable to the agency when it comes to doing research.'

I didn't really need time to think it over but I stayed away from the agency for a couple of weeks so that Mrs. Fitzgerald would know I respected her advice and would think I was giving the situation some consideration.

She hired me and sent me out with a woman called Linda who showed me the ropes. There are three or four other women working full-time for the agency, but I don't see much of them. Mrs. Fitzgerald is my focus and my muse. She gives me my assignments and writes my salary cheques at the end of the month, holding a Parker pen delicately between her plump fingers, the polished tips of her fingers and thumb close to the nib as she writes my name. The good quality, heavy gold rings on her two smallest fingers catch my eye as she spreads her smooth hands slightly to put pressure on the cheque as she tears it from her book. We smile at each other as she passes it to me across the desk. I've always thought I'm lucky to have found her.

I usually explain the late nights I spend following unfaithful lovers by telling my friends I work in a club. It doesn't even really bother me that none of them have ever been curious enough to ask which one or where. Sometimes I tell people I'm a researcher in TV because it's one of those jobs that isn't well paid but means you're making an effort. People think you're interesting enough to talk to in a bar when you tell them what you do, but won't expect you to buy all the drinks. I can talk about the people I meet as if I'd been interviewing them for a documentary.

Taron suggests we meet up in a bar on Coldharbour Lane to talk about the research. She's about my age and looks like Belinda Carlisle circa 1985 or 1986 when the Go-Gos broke up and she lost a little weight before embarking on a solo career. Taron puts all her energies into advertising her beauty and fragility so that you want to protect her. She puts so much care into what she is, she's almost perfect. I find myself telling her my theory that all truly beautiful women have long, arched eyebrows, and we get tipsy on strawberry daiquiris made with real fruit in a liquidizer at the bar. Perhaps I've been living on my own for too long. The mixture of daiquiris and confession is intoxicating and leaves me feeling that I'm more insecure and phoney than she is.

'Are you seeing anyone?' she asks.

'There's a guy I sleep with but it's nothing serious. If I want sex I just call him up and he comes over. We know some of the same people so sometimes we meet by chance and we don't even have sex. That way, each time we go to bed it's like a wonderful idea that's suddenly occurred to us and we're delighted by it. Otherwise I think it would be too clinical.'

I haven't really talked to anyone about him before. I want Taron to see the sex the way I do, as something luminous and exciting, but as I'm telling her about him I'm thinking maybe some days he isn't playing a delicious game, he just doesn't want sex. 'I suppose, if it seems I'm not interested, instead of surging with electric sexual excitement he simply thinks he'll shag me next time. He probably thinks I've got a bad mood or a heavy period.' I imagine him weighing the pros and cons of a tumble under my duvet, supposing my thighs to be slippery with dark blood, not understanding that sex is a shining thing I'm protecting elaborately by playing hard to get. Taron, who has quite small teeth, smiles at me as I think about it. Irrationally, I blame her for puncturing my dream.

We get a cab to my house so we can talk some more. Taron pulls a record cover from my collection and balances it on her knees so she can chop out two thin white lines of coke on it. She doesn't consult me about this. The lines taper at either end. She bends forward and sniffs one of them through a rolled-up note, stopping halfway so she can sniff through the other nostril. She tucks her hair behind her ears to keep it out of the way, even though it isn't long enough to fall on the record cover and trail in the coke. She sniffs and pinches her nose, handing me the record cover and the note. Taron has small paws for hands, with her nails kept short like a child's. She takes less care in maintaining her hands than her clothes or her personality. My aunt used to tell me, 'You must take care of your hands, they're the first thing a man notices.' Taron, with elfin features and a bewitching personality, doesn't need to bother.

'Shall I tell you about my mother?' she asks. 'My mother's a witch. I've known it ever since I was a child, so it doesn't seem strange. She told me that you must never tell people your given name, otherwise someone who knows how to use it will have power over you. A person who keeps their name secret can be very powerful, but the most powerful of all would be an abandoned baby, who would never know the name its mother had chosen for it and so could never tell anyone.

'Lately my mother's become depressed and ill. She's losing the battle against the forces of evil. She says that evil has become organized and power brokers using modern tools are playing into the hands of men with evil powers. She's bought a PC.' With the vision of Taron's mother spending hours in melancholy correspondence with other witches on the Internet, I bend my head and sniff.

'If I can find an abandoned baby, it will help her. It can be her apprentice.' Taron pauses because I'm looking at her oddly, powerless to prevent my eyebrows from drawing up into my hairline. 'I feel guilty. I've never been involved in what she does because I have no power.' She doesn't know that I'm reacting less to her story than to the realization that the record cover says 'Crazy Horses' and I'm wondering whether she's noticed.

'Apparently, babies born with the sac still intact from the womb are protected from drowning. Sailors touch you for luck. I should have been born like that because my mother went into labour without her waters breaking. Lots of mid-wives are witches, and the one who was with my mother must have been a bad one. She produced a glass rod and pierced the sac so her waters broke and I was robbed of my powers. She's told me this story often enough so I'm afraid of water. She used to write me notes to let me off swimming at school because I was sure I'd drown.'

I sniff and taste a bitter flavour on the back of my tongue. I see Taron's mother on a narrow hospital bed, looking like Belinda Carlisle, making small, ineffectual movements with her hands as if to tuck her hair behind her ears, struggling against the pain as her womb contracts to expel a child whom she will warn never to reveal her given name. I see a midwife with big arms step up to the bedside in the poor light with a glass rod in her hands like a wand. I hear her screams of terror and regret as the warm, bloody water flows between her legs and her womb contracts so fiercely that she can see it moving independently under the weak wall of muscles in her belly.

I sniff again. My head is very clear. I feel like a wineglass, with my neck for a stem and my head so clear and round that you could flick it and it would go 'ting'.

'What is your real name?' I ask Taron.

I live in an upside-down house. It's my proudest achievement, something I've wanted since I was a child. Can something be an achievement if someone else builds it and you just buy it from them? The bedroom is on the ground floor, opening onto a small garden. You have to choose between having few visitors or few secrets because you can only get to the garden through the bedroom. The sitting room and the kitchen are upstairs. I've embraced minimalist chic by painting everything white, but the day Taron visits me the room feels empty and soulless. 'Cool,' she says, when we go inside, which makes me feel worse, not better. The tumbling mountain of white pillows in the bedroom looks like a teenager's. I hope she sees that my bleeding heart picture of olive-eyed Jesus on the bedroom wall with his gentle, oval face and flowing, centre-parted hair is supposed to look funky, not pious. I've always thought the driftwood, salvaged from the sea, casting spiky shadows in its final resting place against the stark white walls, looked as if it were twisting in an effort to reach back to the ocean I took it from. Now it looks so...eighties. 'Cool,' she says, her little hands resting for a moment on the smooth wood that now seems to have forgotten about the sea and to be reaching for her as she wanders past to look for a record cover.

The wooden deck floor of the bathroom is painted white; I've slapped white paint on the tongue-and-groove wooden walls, and the window is round like a porthole. You're supposed to believe you're setting sail on the Mediterranean in the bathroom. I can hear Taron clattering about in there, rifling through the bathroom cabinet as I make a cup of tea for us.

When she comes back, I tell her I'll charge her twenty-five pounds an hour for the research. 'Good,' she says, 'that's about the same as the fortune teller is charging me.'

The garden is in darkness. I open the French windows and light citronella candles and put them on the table outside because I want her to see the flowers. I have marguerite daisies and roses in tubs. Tiny, heart-shaped flowers drip from the lateral stems of bleeding heart plants in the borders. I grow celandines next to them, less for their beauty than for the charm of the story that alchemists once used to try and distil gold from their yellow sap. Petals from the apple blossom are scattered on the lawn like confetti.

'I was married once,' Taron tells me. She's smoking Camel Lights. I'm chewing gum and smoking Marlboro Lights. I don't know anyone who smokes full-strength cigarettes anymore.

'It was summer so it was warmer than this. I was wearing a cream-coloured dress. He's French, so beautiful he could have been ripped from the pages of a magazine. He was wearing a cream suit. The fabric made his skin look like mocha chocolate. Confetti caught in his black hair like petals. I didn't realize how much I loved him until after the wedding. I started to worry I'd lose him.'

'What happened to him?'

'Oh...' She waves the words away.

I told Taron about the man I have sex with, but I didn't tell her about my love interest, as it's private. The love is one-sided, all on his side. He's my neighbour and lives in the basement. He says he chose to live in a basement even though it's damp and dark because he's an inventor and it's the proper location for an inventor, in the same way that an attic is the place a starving writer should choose to live. His inventor's mind is the kind that pays attention to very small details, and he expresses his love for me in details, particularly domestic ones.

Sometimes he sits in my kitchen and exudes love for me from every pore while I read out the things in the paper that make me laugh. One day I read that lots of cases of food poisoning are caused by birds pecking at milk bottle tops on doorsteps, so he made me a bottle cover and bird deterrent and left it on my doorstep with a daffodil in it. When I had worked out it wasn't an ugly vase, I had to get up earlier and earlier for a couple of days until I was early enough to catch the Unigate man and ask him to start delivering.

Being loved is a huge responsibility. I think that he was already filled with love before he met me and he just needed a recipient. When he saw me he decided I'd be the one. It's as if he were bewitched in his sleep so he'd fall for the first person he saw when he woke up.

When I get up the morning after Taron comes to the house, I see that he has left me another poem.

The Icing on the Cake

Some people eat the icing on the cake
and discard the marzipan
But I never do

The hardened crust
Of sugar dust
Too sweet for me

The almond paste
Richer in taste
Is softer too

Some people eat the icing on the cake
and discard the marzipan
But I never do

I prefer the marzipan
It makes me think about you

I put it with the others. There are times when his poetry makes me want to put on an apron, cook up a storm and hug his brittle body in my womanly arms. This is one of them, but I'm not very good at cooking so I usually just give him cornflakes sweetened with condensed milk. I don't hug him, either; I only touch the fine hairs on his knuckles very gently and wonder if he has hair on the rest of his body or whether his skin is smooth. I don't like men with hair on their body. I have taken him a cup of tea downstairs and used it to sort of lure him out of the basement and into the light and air in my house where I set the cup on the table and cluck over him for a bit to show I don't think he's weird for leaving a poem for me.

'Jeff,' I say, not mentioning the poetry, 'so what are you working on at the moment?' His sallow face lights up and he talks animatedly.

'You know how when you watch an advert on TV or see a billboard and you're not sure if it's for a Range Rover or the Marlboro Man or for chewing gum or Diet Sprite? And you know how cigarette companies have had to get so cryptic they don't even mention the product, you just know what they're selling because of the colours they use?'

'Yes.'

'Well, I've been thinking about this, and I think it would be possible to distil the essence of every advert into one that could represent just about any product. It would be so powerful that everyone who saw it could want to buy a different product.'

'One advert would advertise every product in the world?'

'Yes.'

We think about this idea for a while. I reach out and touch the hairs on another of his knuckles, very gently.

'Won't the people in the advertising industry mind?' I ask, but I know it's an irrelevant question. Jeff invents things to solve a problem, simplify life or eradicate unnecessary labour. He dreams of a world in which none of us have to work, without realizing that we only do it because we have to get money somehow. I look out of the window at the early morning sunshine and share his utopian dreams for a moment. I wonder if he will ever be able to invent something that will make my job redundant.

'They could get work in a related field,' he says. 'They might want to go into films.'

'So what will your ad be like?'

'I'm still working on the formula, but I think you can work out the elements that it needs, the way you can for a song. It has to haunt you. When you watch it, you have to feel there's something missing in your life.'

'When I was little I used to spend ages chasing the reflection of the sunlight on the kitchen floor. It didn't matter whether I ran fast or stalked it or tried jumping, it still stayed just ahead of me.'

'Elusive.'

'Yes. You have to want the product as much as I wanted to catch the sunlight. You need background music that moves you. Something from the past. You need one of those anthems that they use on the Levi's ads.' I warm up and start to get excited. So everyone in the advertising industry may have to take a very long holiday if Jeff succeeds. So who cares? 'When that beautiful man dives through all the swimming pools and the song is "Mad About the Boy", I'm so consumed with desire that I don't know if I should buy the swimming pool or the music or the jeans or the advertising agency.'

'I'm going to choose something from the seventies or the eighties. I've got Annie Lennox in mind because her voice is pure and her songs make me feel sad. I like the one about the angel.'

Sometimes I think Jeff and I reveal too much about ourselves in these chats. Now he knows about the sunlight on the kitchen floor and that I get turned on by a half-naked male model in a swimming pool, and I know he's sentimental and gets sad when he listens to Annie Lennox. I wonder if he's gay and then I remember he's in love with me. His emotions are very delicate. I'm glad I'm the first person he saw when he woke up after being bewitched.

'What are you going to do today, Ali?' He usually calls me Ali. I suppose you could spell it Allie, Ally or Ali, but I prefer the version used by the boxer and I spell it that way in my head when I hear the word.

I tell him I don't know, I think I will take it easy today because I have to start temping next week. There is an emotion that crosses his face too briefly for me to be sure whether it is a look of suffering. When it's gone he's frowning in sympathy. He knows I hate the work.

I like being a detective because I don't want to work in an office, but I sometimes go undercover as a secretary to spy on men who are having affairs or to check the security of information in a company. People who work in offices are crazy, and they create an environment they hate, write rules they want to break, cast each other in roles they despise. It's like they're sixth formers in an end-of-term drama acting out the agony of everything they fear most in their life, but they forget to end the play. 'How I hate working here,' they say. 'How lucky you are to be a temp. I work such long hours but I never get paid for it. I never see my family, I can't relax on holiday, my hair is falling out, and I'm getting fat.' *Why don't you stop, then, if it makes you unhappy?* I wonder. Call for someone to turn up the house lights, blink from the stage and step off into a new life. Do something that interests you. Sometimes I think that perhaps they enjoy their work, and the language they use is a shorthand for expressing their happiness. Perhaps there is an argot that I haven't got the hang of, like when people on children's TV say 'wicked' and 'bad' when they mean that something is good. When people in offices say, 'I work such long hours but I never get paid for it,' perhaps they mean, 'I'm really valuable to this company, people can't manage without me.' Or if they say, 'I never see my family,' they mean, 'See how attractive I am, my wife still loves me even though I ignore her except to talk about work.'

A common language is very important in social situations. People use jargon at work to impress each other, but they also use the same catchphrases as the boss so that they will fit in. Sometimes they mimic the boss so much that I think they're taking the piss and I get frightened and awed and giggly when the boss is in earshot until I realize they're just sucking up. Then I come home feeling empty, and I talk to Jeff for a long time until I feel filled up again.

Today we talk about some more about advertisements. There's a print advert for a pregnancy testing kit that shows a couple in a rowing boat looking overjoyed. I say it always makes me want to have a baby because of the emotion they've captured in the photo, and that's clever because usually people only buy the kit when they're worried about whether to get an abortion. We both like the Tango ads, although we don't drink fizzy drinks. I only really like water and Jeff drinks a lot of milk, although that's linked to my arrangement with the Unigate man.

'Brixton invaded by Japanese knotweed,' I read from the local paper. 'A plant controlled by law in Britain because it grows more than forty millimetres per day between April and August, destroying plant life, roads and pavements, has been spotted in the Brixton area. A task force has been mobilized to tackle the problem, and people are urged to report further sightings to Brixton's senior park ranger.' I note down the number before I throw away the newspaper. Jeff and I are quiet for a while, quiet enough to hear the rustling of the voracious knotweed if it were growing nearby. There is only the distant sound of a plane, taking the scenic route along the Thames as it comes in to land at Heathrow. The day is clear enough for the passengers to be able to make out the flowerbeds at the roundabout near Battersea Park, if they are looking out of the window. I look up out of my window and watch the white trail the plane leaves in the sky.

'That's one point six millimetres an hour,' comments Jeff. He's smiling. He reminds me of the picture of Jesus in my bedroom, except that his teeth are crooked so he looks roguish when he smiles. Jesus isn't smiling; he's looking enigmatic and gentle as you would expect from a man who will soon die for the sins of the world. The other difference is that Jeff doesn't have a beard. Jeff and the Jesus in the picture are probably about the same age, which is twenty-nine years old. Another connection is that they both have a mission to save the world, although Jesus had more potential for disappointment ('My God, why have you forsaken me?') as the scale of his project was more ambitious.

'Jeff, what else are you working on?' I ask, to underline the difference between the two men in my own mind.

'I thought I might try adapting a time-controlled cat feeder to help people on diets or giving up smoking spliff so the lid pops open at intervals to reveal a Mars bar, or a ready-rolled spliff.'

'I think whoever invented the coating for Peanut M&M's must feel very proud. They never melt, even when you eat them in the summer. I remember when I was really little I used to leave Smarties at the bottom of the garden for the fairies, and the colours would smudge and fade in the rain.'

'They have blue ones now.'

'I know.'

3

The Agency

ELLA FITZGERALD SITS at her desk with her hands folded on a buff-coloured file marked 'Project Brown Dog', considering its contents. She breathes evenly, and her plump, smooth hands are still, her handsome features composed. Momentarily distracted from Project Brown Dog, Mrs. Fitzgerald wonders whether you are supposed to be able to feel something when you're thinking.

She's aware of a distinct tingling sensation when she concentrates. She's able to pinpoint a physical process starting simultaneously at either side of her head just at her temples, corresponding to the place where the muscles attach to her jaw and which she can feel moving when she clenches her back teeth together or when she practices the teeth sucking noise of disrespect that black people make. When she focuses and thinks hard, Mrs. Fitzgerald reflects, the sensation seems to move from the sides to a central position high in her head.

She's outwardly at ease with herself, which is why young, troubled women like Alison find her presence reassuring. Mrs. Fitzgerald has the appearance of being able to deal with any matter, domestic or business, with equanimity. There is no Mr. Fitzgerald. A solicitor who specialized in representing the underdog, he died prematurely, leaving his young wife with a small office in Brixton and a network of left-wing contacts in the investigative world. Mrs. Fitzgerald never remarried. She has carefully audited her life and found she has no requirement for a husband.

The office is warm, perhaps a little stuffy. The light isn't quite right; the windows are small and nearer the ceiling than the floor, so the sunlight entering the room leaves dark corners and shadows that aren't corrected by turning on the overhead light. Ella moves her right hand across the file on her desk, then moves her right hand across the top of her left, recording the difference between touching something and simultaneously touching and being touched. There is a difference, she notes, between the sensation of touching in each case, apparently caused by the distracting messages that being touched sends to the brain. A more scientific way of approaching the problem would be to compare the sensation of touching her own hand and touching someone else's hand. It is important to compare like with like in such cases, but the opportunity does not present itself to Mrs. Fitzgerald in her office, and her professional relationship with Alison does not permit her to approach her with the problem in the next room.

Project Brown Dog is an operation for which Mrs. Fitzgerald has taken personal responsibility. 'You can be assured of my personal attention,' she told the client, 'as chief investigator.'

Alison's imminent involvement is part of her strategy. Alison looked with interest at the folder on her desk when Mrs. Fitzgerald permitted her hands to flutter from its surface so that Alison could read its title. The 'Top Secret' stamp in the corner is an uncharacteristically frivolous indulgence. It is important that Alison should want to work on the project with her, that she respect the client's need for total confidentiality. Initially the work will be routine, but Mrs. Fitzgerald suspects that Alison will be flattered enough by the invitation to work with her, and her enthusiasm will carry them even if things get nasty. And they could get nasty.

Mrs. Fitzgerald's brother Clive haunts the office on days when he can find nothing else to distract him. He monopolizes the phone and spends too long in the toilet, disturbing the comfortable, female environment. Linda, whispering just within earshot, explains him to newcomers as 'Creepy Clive.'

There are copies of *Vogue*, *Elle*, *Cosmo* and *Marie Claire* in the reception. Mrs. Fitzgerald knows she could pick up a copy of *Cosmo* and read ten ways to tell if your lover is cheating, ten ways to improve your sex life, ten ways towards a new winter wardrobe, but never ten ways to tell if you are mad. Mrs. Fitzgerald secretly fears that she's being claimed by madness, as her brother is. For the moment, she's troubled by nothing more than fanciful thoughts, but she has taken a number of measures to avoid the next stage. She does not mention Clive's aberrations to anyone else; she even seems to fail to notice them. People wonder if the usually perceptive Mrs. Fitzgerald is blind to her brother's faults. Even if they hint that Clive is a little strange, she gives no sign that she has noticed. She believes that the way to combat her own descent into the void is to deny that her brother has any problems, as if something is only real if you believe in it.

It is fairly well documented that when schizophrenics hear voices they commonly describe hearing a middle-aged male BBC presenter. A less well-known fact is that mental patients often mistook Princess Diana for Moors murderess Myra Hindley when she visited them, which upset her. Clive's world is crowded with ancient, wise ethnic minorities that no one else can see. This does not mean he's disturbed, although Mrs. Fitzgerald finds it peculiar.

Ella picks up the phone to call her brother, then reconsiders and places the receiver in the cradle. At this time of day he likes to commune with the spirit world from a church in Marylebone Road. He practised for many months before he was able to make meaningful contact with lost souls from the other side and was delighted when he eventually succeeded. 'Pick a card,' Clive said to Mrs. Fitzgerald one day, surprising her by brandishing a pack of playing cards in her office. 'Pick a card,' he insisted. He explained that he would be able to guess the card she held in her hand because a dead Red Indian was standing behind her and looking over her shoulder. *Native American,* Ella thought. *If he's there, he'll prefer to be called a Native American.* Clive got the card right.

These days Clive keeps his new friends to himself, although occasionally Ella glances up and catches him looking intently off to one side, as if at some invisible presence. She suspects he's just doing it for show, to draw attention to himself. He always had difficulty making and keeping friends. Why should the dead be any different? If they are contactable, why would they waste their time playing card tricks with Clive when they could be brokering world peace with presidents?

Clive is a clever man but highly strung. He doesn't seem interested in work and Mrs. Fitzgerald isn't sure how he manages for money although he claims to have an income from investing in the stock market, and he bets on horses when he gets a tip from the spirit world. She hopes he's luckier with that than he is with scratch cards. If she leaves him alone in the office, she often returns to little grey piles of dust on her desk where he's frantically uncovered the unmatching boxes with a coin before discarding the cards in her wastepaper bin. *If I had a pound for every one of those,* Mrs. Fitzgerald thinks grimly.

His family believed Clive was destined for greatness when he transcended his ordinary background to go to Cambridge, but he spent his time with other highly strung young men who cultivated rather than discouraged his madness, and when he failed his foreign office entry exams he never really recovered. The young men who whispered nonsense together in 1960 have faded into middle age and are scattered across the continents in important jobs with the foreign office and the military, although Clive still hears from them and they still whisper together because Mrs. Fitzgerald catches him on the phone to them sometimes. If she knew the identity of the men he conspires with, she'd be very distressed.

Mrs. Fitzgerald runs her fingers over the warm wood of her desk and thinks about giving up the agency and moving away from Clive and his ghosts. *If I could live anywhere,* she thinks, *I would like to live in Torquay and grow palm trees.* Palm trees might disappoint her with their slow rate of growth in genteel Torquay, the spiky foliage raising skywards almost imperceptibly year after year. She grows camellias, a magnolia, begonias, roses and fuchsias in her garden in Brixton, favouring fragrant or showy, fragile blossoms. She loves her garden. Late at night, when there is something troubling her in her mind, when the spirit world is awake and most of London is asleep, Mrs. Fitzgerald has occasionally seen a fox walking on the lawn in the moonlight. The fox, like Mrs. Fitzgerald, has adapted to urban living and is usually on its way to scavenge for the remains of a Marks & Spencer ready meal in her dustbin.

Mrs. Fitzgerald has read somewhere that if you have fox or badger mess in your garden, then the only way to stop them using the garden as a lavatory is to deposit the faeces from a larger predator there. This she took to mean that you should defecate in your own garden to stop other creatures leaving their filth. It is not something she has ever been tempted to try. She has also read that if you plant lilies in your garden it will stop ghosts walking there. Red lilies, yellow lilies, white lilies, orange lilies shine their fiery full-of-life colours in her borders from July to September. If the charm works, her garden should be free of ghosts in the summer.

4

Infidelity

I HAVE A COUPLE of cases on at the moment. A woman says her cat has been stolen by neighbours and tells me she's seen it staring with what she calls a plaintive expression from their upstairs window. I've also got some infidelity investigations going.

When I take a case where the man is having an affair, I always visit the wife in her home. What does she want from the investigation? If the case corresponds to an executive affair pattern—and it usually does—the wife only wants a risk assessment. There are always wifely photos of her in an Alice band at the side of a tallish man in a suit. When we meet, her hair is usually several shades darker than in the photo, her face thinner and slightly drawn, but she's still dressed as if for a day at the office. We talk about how difficult it is bringing up three children under five years old. She's usually buckling under the strain of the last one. She's struggling with finding space for the car seats for three babies, with three different kinds of meals to prepare (plus something for him when he gets home), different sleeping patterns for the children, little sleep for herself. We talk, casually, about the difficulty of finding time for romance. The wife rarely cares, frankly, if he is shagging someone. It may even be a relief. A few more guilt presents, a little less physical bother at the weekends. If he's no longer interested in fiddling about with her, it's OK now to stick the baby in bed with them to keep it quiet.

The wife wants to know, what's the girlfriend like? Is she common, available, dispensable? Or is she a younger blonde with an Alice band? Does she make him happy or is she after his upmarket sperm and an expensive house to breed it in? Will he stay or go? I don't mean that the wife doesn't love him. She does, usually. She's had to make some concessions, though. He might work long hours and bring more work home with him. Perhaps he travels abroad every month, or every week. He's losing his hair or getting a bit fatter. Of course she loves him. It's like buying something you like very much in the shops, an antique dresser or a very pretty necklace, but once you've got it home the shop-keeper keeps coming round and saying, 'Actually, I know I said it was a hundred and twenty pounds, but I've decided I'd rather have a hundred and thirty pounds. Can you give me another ten pounds?' And then another ten pounds and another ten pounds. So when you first find your hus-band, it's OK that he works long hours; it seems that his love is worth the price of seeing him sometime after nine o'clock at night. But then someone takes his weekends, his hair, his sense of humour. Now there is a knock at the door and someone else wants to take away the sex, or make you share it with them. The wife loves him, the puny man in the suit, even though he's not worthy of her. She only hopes he has found someone who is ordinary and common to suck his cock, rather than a soft-looking blonde in an Alice band whose womb is twitching because she's pushing thirty. They forget that he has aged as much as they have, that he's lucky to get anyone to do it with him, no matter what their hairstyle. But then I'm forgetting that men often get lucky. I forget that I'm pushing thirty and would probably fuck their husband if he fancied me, even though I know it's a sin to sleep with a married man.

In different cases I meet later versions of the same women. They're still paying their ten pounds for something that has long since lost its value. It is the same concept as women on council estates who buy from catalogues and are still paying twenty-two pence a week for something they bought so long ago that it is broken or has been nicked. By now they are paying the metaphorical ten pounds for the children. The children do hard drugs and smuggle them. Sometimes they demonstrate the contempt for women they've learned from their mothers by beating their wives.

My investigations often involve going undercover in the company where the husband works. I get quite a lot of work through personal recommendation so I explain to the wife that on no account should she discuss my methods with her friends or family. One day they may need me to help, and how can they do that if they've told their husband how I work?

One growth area in our industry is vetting neighbours for potential house buyers now that the housing market is supposedly picking up again. Over the past seven years there have been seventeen suicides and murders in Britain because of noise disputes, so it's not as crazy as it sounds.

Mrs. Fitzgerald is heading up a surveillance and research operation code-named Project Brown Dog and she's asked me to work with her on it. She's being mysterious about it. We don't usually have code names for the work we're doing.

'Women operatives in this industry have to prove themselves more than men,' she tells me sternly. 'Do you remember the McLibel case? The young woman investigator had an affair with the man she was watching. It was the same with Deborah Winger and Tom Berenger when she was supposed to be investigating racial-hate murders. The public's perception is that women are weak and easily seduced. I'm proud that my organization is not seen like that.'

I'm not sure where this preamble is leading us. Does she think I'm likely to have sex with one of the people we're watching? Men hardly fall over themselves to get to me when I'm undercover. The whole point is to avoid drawing attention to myself. Sometimes as I walk to work early in the morning, men in vans make it clear that I only have to say the word and they'll do it to me. But I don't think that really counts as I'm never in the mood, and anyway I think they shout out to all the women they pass on their route. 'Lovely tits,' one of them shouted this morning. Or was it 'Low tits'? When I thought about it I realized I didn't care.

'We have been assigned a very sensitive task,' interrupts Mrs. Fitzgerald. 'We have been asked to investigate some suspicious activity on the southwest coast. It may be nothing, but signs indicate that something unethical or illegal is happening. An old enemy of mine has been hired to put up a ring of misinformation around this activity and monitor security leaks. That usually means something pretty serious is going on.'

'Your enemy?' I picture Mrs. Fitzgerald duelling at a waterfall, like Sherlock Holmes with Moriarty.

'Well, he's not my enemy, technically. He's an investigator like us, although he calls his organization a business intelligence agency and traditionally accepts the kind of work I won't touch, and so we find ourselves on opposing sides.'

'Who's hired us?'

'I can't tell you. If I told you, it might put you in danger. You need to know more about the kind of people we're up against, though. Did you know there's an agency that has earned around three million pounds taking photographs of the Newbury Bypass protesters and compiling dossiers of information about them?'

Mrs. Fitzgerald's ethics do not permit her to get involved in such malarkey. She would take money from the protesters if they had any, but of course they don't. She takes a pile of labelled photographs of two men from the folder in front of her and peels them off one by one, slapping them face up in front of me on the desk as if she's dealing tarot cards. 'Flower,' she says, 'and Bird, my old adversary. Their services have been retained by Emphglott, a pharmaceutical company that specializes in vivisection and genetic manipulation in animals. They recently broke the legs of thirty-seven beagles without anaesthetic to test a new drug that's supposed to heal broken bones.'

'Why didn't they use anaesthetic? Or why didn't they just get dogs that were already injured? There are loads of them on *Animal Hospital*.'

'Exactly.' Evidently, I have said the right thing. 'Do you know the significance of the code name Brown Dog?' My silence indicates that I do not, but I'm reluctant to admit it and spoil the mood of mutual understanding I have created with the *Animal Hospital* quip.

'The Brown Dog died at the hands of vivisectionists in University College in 1903. He'd been subjected to experiments for two months, handed from one vivisectionist to another. His treatment caused public outrage. There's a statue commemorating him at the edge of a shady path in Battersea Park. I'd like to think we've learned our lessons from 1903 and moved on so that we treat animals ethically, with dignity and respect, but I know it doesn't happen.'

She slaps a last photo onto the desk, a picture of a pinched-faced woman in her forties. 'Miss Lester, director of services at Emphglott. My client would like to know what Miss Lester is up to in some supposedly abandoned government buildings in the West Country, and so would I, Alison.'

I have never seen Mrs. Fitzgerald so impassioned. Well, whatever floats her boat. It's interesting when you find out what someone cares about. I stare at her for a bit until she catches me, then I look away.

5

Covent Garden

CLIVE IS SULKING because Mrs. Fitzgerald has asked him to pop out and buy some stationery. He travels all the way into the West End, as if there are no pens and paper to be had in Brixton. He's exasperated by the lack of respect he gets at the agency and is on a mission to get it elsewhere, which usually means anywhere you part with a great deal of money, like a betting shop or indeed any kind of shop in Covent Garden. He goes into Jigsaw in Floral Street to buy a zippered cardigan, attracted by the firm fishermen's knit stitches and suede trim of the garment in the window display.

The shop assistant notices he appears to be seeking advice about the cardigan from someone as he walks out of the changing cubicle to check his reflection. The two men are alone in the shop as it's still early morning. 'What do you think?' says Clive, pulling the hem of the cardigan down at the back, adjusting the line so it sits well on his shoulders. He's startled by the murmured, half-hearted flattery from the young assistant, whose advice he had not been seeking. The assistant couldn't know that Clive brings invisible companions from the spirit world to provide critical advice and support on shopping expeditions. Sometimes they help out by switching the price tags, but Clive doesn't think it's appropriate on this occasion. The cardigan is such a handsome item of clothing that the price seems justified. 'I'll take it,' he says. The assistant takes some tissue paper and a paper bag from under the counter and begins to wrap. His features arrange into an expression that could be read as pure concentration, or as respect.

6

Dick, Flower & Bird

DICK MASTERS SITS at his desk with his clippings, pasting another story into the scrapbook. It is quite a laborious process because newspaper cuttings discolour and fade after a while, so the trick is to take a photocopy and paste that in, discarding the newspaper original. Dick supposes there is an irony in this process and experiments with inventing or converting aphorisms to suit the task. *Discard before discolour,* he tries, as he dabs at the paper with Copydex. He doesn't really like that one. He's never understood why anyone would choose death before dishonour. The preservation of human life is paramount. He formulates another.

Out with the old, in with the news, he thinks, as the newspaper, leaf-like, drifts from his fingers to the bin. The work is boring, but Dick finds he can absorb himself in it if he runs a mental commentary. This is to make up for the office banter he imagines would surround him if he worked with other people all day.

Dick is collecting evidence about the madness and evil orchestrated by the world of commerce. He pays attention to minor infractions of civil liberty as well as the terrible injustices inflicted on the poor and the disenfranchised. When he reads about people being poisoned, choked, starved, experimented on and stopped too often for driving a fancy car, he puts the story in his scrapbook. When he reads in the newspapers that convicted drunk drivers are being targeted in a direct mail campaign by businesses offering tailored services that fit their crime (cabs home from the pub and DIY breathalysers), he makes the connection that someone in the justice system has sold a list to someone in business, and he cuts the story from the newspaper. It feels amateurish and painstaking but it gives him a picture of what is happening in the world. Dick sees conspiracy wherever he looks. He believes that someone, somewhere is in charge of the bad things in the world. If he can find them and stop them, he will make everything all right. But even wicked people are stumbling around just trying to get along. They aren't involved in an interdependent network. If you cut one of them down, another will come along.

Most people think only of beauty when buying a bunch of flowers. Dick worries about the chemicals used in flower production in Colombia which cause miscarriages and premature birth. Most people think they've got a bargain when they buy a cheap T-shirt. Dick worries about the children missing school to operate the looms. Having a social conscience is quite burdensome and it doesn't leave Dick much time for a social life, even though he'd like one.

Dick cares about civil liberty and human rights violations around the world, the misuse of political power and intrusion on privacy. For fundraising purposes, he spends a lot of time researching the mistreatment of animals. His organization relies on donations and subscriptions to newsletters to run its operation and animals pull in a lot of money.

Dick has a large, round head with short hair. He looks like a Kewpie doll, although he doesn't know this. He is intelligent enough to get a job that would earn him good money, but too clever to want one. The organization he has joined has very few operatives, so he outsources a lot of their work. The surveillance work is handled by Mrs. Fitzgerald's female detective agency in Brixton.

A teenager has given birth to a baby at a high school dance in America, put the body in a rubbish bin, then returned to the dance floor. The first anyone knows of the incident, according to the newspaper report, is the next day when a cleaner empties the bins. Dick is less interested in the question that appears to be troubling the reporter— whether the baby lived for a while after being born—than what was in the baby-mother's mind as she painfully delivered the enormous, bloody thing. Dead or alive, what difference does it make now? And what did the cleaner think, doing a nasty job, mopping up the teenage vomit, the smouldered roaches from the joints smoked in the toilets, the splashes of piss from careless boys? Dick imagines the cleaner has been thinking that nothing could be worse than cleaning the detritus after young people have been having fun. Then the arresting experience of something unfamiliarly heavy among the paper towels in the bin—something lifeless and gory like the bag of giblets when you're making an effort for Sunday dinner. What made the cleaner investigate rather than incinerate? Perhaps the faintest hope that it could be something nice in there, heavy in the bin. Dick does not collect this story; it sheds no light on the murky corners of the world he is researching.

For Dick, the world of commerce is a place in which people subsume their personalities to an organization in return for money, an organization that makes them work too many hours a day and sends them on 'personal development' courses to reengineer their personalities. Dick doesn't know that people quite enjoy living like this, having their goals written and evaluated for them by someone else, attuning the rhythm of their lives to commercial banking hours rather than daylight and night-time, summer and autumn.

Dick would like to free them from the comfort of their daily routine, their guaranteed income, their pleasant, light offices and their flowering and failing office romances. He'd like to throw open all the windows of the offices in London so their inhabitants can fly away and be free. He'd push them from the crowded windowsills. 'Be free' (splat), 'be free' (thud, splat). He doesn't see they don't have wings. Only the more junior members of such organizations would be spared, the ignominious ground floor desks and windowless offices proving to be their salvation. Even so, even though he is obsessive and misguided, Dick has a point. There are companies who collect and exchange information about their staff and use it to make decisions about hiring or promoting them. They set up help lines and monitor them; they install nurses in their buildings and analyse their employees' urine. Agencies provide the companies with information about the parking tickets their staff have collected, petitions they've signed, who they slept with as a student, who their wife sleeps with.

A bright chap of around thirty-five, married with two children and a house in Surrey, might find an agency has sent a confidential report to a headhunter suggesting he is 'an unstable homosexual with left-wing sympathies and links to animal rights groups' because he went to a public school where it was not unusual for a boy to have a fling with another boy to take the edge off teen angst, because his wife has the *Guardian* delivered, because his children signed a petition at the Body Shop on a family trip hunting for antiques in Brighton. Companies often pay to find out more when they read 'unstable', it's a teaser. The report-writers have justified it on this occasion because the bright chap had a poem published when he was at university and he has just applied for a very large mortgage.

Dick's activities are focused on damage-limitation, spoiler tactics and fact-finding. He is playing a dangerous game because of the money involved. Mrs. Fitzgerald is playing with him. Soon Alison will play, too.

Dick picks up the phone to call Mrs. Fitzgerald. As a capable woman who is his ally in the fight against evil, Dick finds it reassuring to call her every now and then and hear her measured voice, her careful words. He would not find it helpful to know that as he rings, Mrs. Fitzgerald in her office in Brixton fears that she is being claimed by madness. Struck increasingly by fanciful thoughts, she cannot ask other people if they have the same experiences in case they, too, draw the conclusion that she is mad. Instead, she works hard at appearing controlled, considered, fair, sane.

'Mrs. Fitzgerald?' Dick is really surprised at how pleased he is to be speaking aloud to someone. He feels suddenly very lonely. Mrs. Fitzgerald is a great strength, his comrade-in-arms.

'Dick.' The sound of the phone ringing has arrested Ella's fingers where they gently stroked the desk. Dick, she'd like to say, do you sometimes feel a heightened sense of self-consciousness to the extent that everything else seems unreal? Would you say that if you are part of a world that is unreal that you must be unreal? Do you sometimes feel that you are gripped by madness?

'Dick,' she says warmly, 'I'm glad you called. I've just finished briefing Alison. She's fully on board with Brown Dog.'

Dick and Mrs. Fitzgerald are currently monitoring the activities of business intelligence agencies with names like Control Inter and LimitForce One that seem to have flowed from the pens of *Thunderbirds* script-writers and that have been designed to appeal to men who drive fast cars. They are fronted by two well-connected men who used to be in the army called Major Flower and Major General Bird and populated by shady former Metropolitan policemen who are not prepared to reveal their names.

Major Flower likes to think he is in charge at Control Inter, but he has been hired because his title looks cute on company literature and because he is good-looking in an Ivanhoe kind of a way. He is also irrepressibly cheerful and enthusiastic about everything, so he is very popular with customers and personnel, especially the younger ones. Major Flower may not be in charge, but he earns lots of money. He has quite a bit of free time during the day, so every Friday he spends some of his enormous salary on a present for his wife and goes home early to take it to her.

Major General Bird is in charge of his outfit, there is no doubt about that. He has a patrician nose and a stern demeanour. People sometimes say his nose is like a beak, but this is only because of his name. If the BBC commissioned another TV series about a grumpy, maverick police inspector, ran out of actors, and asked respected television news presenter Jeremy Paxman to play the lead, then the overall impression would be something like the one given by Major General Bird.

He thinks he is a decent man, but in his career he has learned that you cannot trust the enemy; that you must strike first to be sure of winning; that there are nasty, hidden rooms under the Thames where a fine line is drawn between interrogation and torture. In this job, Bird thinks of Dick, Mrs. Fitzgerald and Alison as the enemy, and therefore if he were to hear they'd been sprayed with rubber bullets as they walked in Battersea Park one day, Bird would not have the crisis of conscience to be expected from the real Jeremy Paxman. Bird has a lot of international experience. When he was working as an adviser to the government in Indonesia, he introduced the idea of using snakes for crowd control and to obtain confessions from suspects.

Flower and Bird's organizations are information-intensive. This means they need lots of information to do their job properly. They collect it from a variety of sources and use poorly paid records clerks to record and sort it. While the main source of their income is information gathering, in some circumstances they are also hired to protect commercially sensitive information or assess the risk of it being leaked to someone like Dick.

The Church of Jesus Christ of Latter-day Saints, or Mormons, encourages its members to contribute the details of their family trees to a centralized list. It is a fundamental tenet of their faith that those who didn't have the opportunity to join the church while alive can earn its blessings by proxy, through the efforts of living relatives, while they wait in the afterlife. The list is a very useful resource for genealogists. Business intelligence agencies have a similar resource that documents the living, and if hell existed it might be a very useful first stopping point for interested parties from the fires of the underworld on a recruitment drive in the UK. This database lists all the criminals and their misdemeanours, all political activists, people who ring premium rate numbers for advice about sexually transmitted diseases, and people who write to newspapers.

'Are you against racism? Would you like to sign a petition?' Tall young men with good teeth and Socialist Worker badges pester people on the streets as they bump their shopping on their thighs on busy Saturdays before Christmas. These are usually amateurs working for organizations like Bird's and Flower's. They might even be Bird's children, making themselves useful in a gap year before university. The petitions are not intended for influential MPs; they are sent straight to a central location for entry onto a database. The young people work on a piecework basis without much supervision, paid a few pence for each name they submit, so they sometimes employ underhand techniques more usually associated with high-pressure salesmen. They place adverts in newspapers and magazines: 'Have you ever done something illegal? Do you have a story to tell? Call researcher in confidence.' They run 'whistle-blower' phone lines and hack into advice lines to produce lists of 'undesirables.' One enterprising individual sent his younger siblings out onto his local estate with a sponsored swim form, and when they returned with the lists of names and addresses, he submitted those, too.

This amateur information-gathering sideline is quite separate from the lucrative intelligence work done by skilled professionals. Professionals target suspicious individuals, watch them, search their homes, intimidate their families if necessary, then provide detailed reports on their status. They operate in cells, working independently from each other on a 'need-to-know' basis to minimize leaks and crises of conscience from employees.

The custodians of the lists of names submitted by the amateurs and forwarded to the professionals are the records clerks, working in ill-paid isolation from other members of their organizations. For security reasons, they do not have access to sensitive information or the ability to interpret the data. Only the man at the top ever needs to know every-thing.

Bird and Flower share information with each other sometimes. They have access to similar networks and buy secrets from the same people. Dick knows what they're doing, and they know all about him. It can be a claustro-phobic environment where lives criss-cross and business intrudes on family. Bird's sister-in-law knows a girl who got drunk at a party and slept with Flower a long time ago, before he married his wife. Dick's girlfriend went to school with Bird's receptionist.

Bird, his eyes on the photo of his muscular Boxer dog leaping to catch a Frisbee, picks up the phone to talk to Flower. Bird is an animal lover but finds it easy enough to square this with his work for Emphglott. After all, he only loves his own dog, not every mangy mutt in the world. He isn't Rolf Harris, crying on *Animal Hospital.*

As he listens to the hypnotic ringing tone of the phone, his eyes unfocus slightly and move from the Boxer dog to a crystal trophy in his glass-fronted cabinet. Two supplicat-ing hands cup a carved flame. The trophy is usually only

awarded to prize-winning dogs in the championship sponsored annually by Emphglott, but Bird was presented with
a reproduction by an Emphglott executive who spotted the
photo in Bird's office. The picture is conspicuous because
it doesn't compete for desk space with photos of Bird's wife
or children. 'The images of their faces are emblazoned on
my heart; I don't need pictures,' he explains patiently to
anyone who comments on the absence of family photos in
his office. Most people are too shy to ask.

'Flower, I need you to be on the alert for me. There are
saboteurs who are attacking vegetable patches around the
world. They're dangerous terrorists and their vandalism is
escalating. They're very well organized. We know they have
a list of targets. I'd like to get my hands on the list.'

'Vegetables?'

'Genetically altered vegetables. My client, Emphglott—'

'Dog people?'

'Well, they're probably best known for their work with
dogs; they sponsor the dog show. As a matter of fact, they
research scientific advances into all aspects of animal hus-
bandry. They're currently pioneering genetic research on
animals. The thing I'd like to find out, Flower, is whether
Emphglott is on the hit list, or whether the terrorists are
restricting themselves to vegetables. Dick Masters and his
animal protectionists have hired the Fitzgerald woman
again. I'm not sure yet whether her brief is to monitor
Emphglott or to take action of some kind, but she's put her
best agent on the case.'

'Who's that?'

'Woman called Alison Temple. Apparently also uses the
name Wonderland. Divorcee. If Dick Masters knows the

extent of the genetic experimentation Emphglott is under-taking, if he's going to coordinate the saboteurs to target Emphglott and Emphglott are on the hit list, he will have shared that information with Mrs. Fitzgerald. I've got a con-tact at Fitzgerald's agency and I'm going to try and find out whether the saboteurs are coming after Emphglott. "Discre-tion Assured" be damned. There's a lot of money at stake here. If you hear anything or see anything, let me know.'

7

The Shig

THERE IS A CREATURE that lives in paradise on disused Ministry of Defence land near Weymouth, rooting among the dabs of colour in the field where wild flowers grow. It is called a shig. There are so many butterflies on the land that eyes are drawn at first to the dazzling yellows or blues flickering as their wings move among the wild flowers. But another, closer look reveals the fattest, woolliest animal on earth, the product of a union between a pig and a sheep. Its size is as remarkable as its ancestry, because it is as big as a small van, never having stopped growing since it was first bred, in great secrecy, on land that used to house the underwater weapons research buildings where scientists built missiles for nuclear submarines during the Cold War. The shig's fleece is a lustrous mass of golden curls. When it is slaughtered for its delicious meat, there will be no bristles to shave, only fleece to be shorn. The shig's existence is significant less for the attributes of the creature itself—nice meat, nice wool—than for the fact that it proves that animals can be bred across species. Now the scientists responsible for the creature face two problems: first, it has proved impossible to breed from it. Second, the keeper is so attached to it that he's going to be reluctant to give up the beast for slaughter when the time comes.

There have been other, less successful experiments in the past. A pow, bred for meat, leather and milk, was notable for its attractive, snouty face and curly tail, but its stunted legs caused its udder to drag unhygienically on the ground. A dig, a fierce fighting creature, had to be destroyed because of its snarling ruthlessness and propensity to attack whoever came near it, even if they were bringing it food. There was a rumour that it was to be sold on the black market as a 'digbull' to violent men of low intelligence as part of a programme to deter these men from procreating. The pets were to be encouraged to turn on them and savage their private parts. In the end, according to the rumour-mongers, it was agreed that the dig was too vicious and unpredictable to be released commercially, and the eugenics programme would continue using pit bulls and Dobermans.

Only the shig remains, a beautiful if overlarge example of man's triumphant meddling with the fabric of the universe. The initial process to produce this example of mixed breeding was complex and fraught with failure. The gene was put into a newly fertilized egg cell called a blastocyst and the embryo planted in a surrogate mother Merino sheep. The shig is female because scientists mapped her gender characteristics from her mother. As was the case with Dolly the cloned sheep, it is only possible to produce more female shigs using genetic science. The future of the species will not be assured until the shig can be persuaded to breed, as continued cloning will produce a species that isn't resistant to disease. Many attempts to fertilize the shig with sperm created under laboratory conditions have proved futile. There's a long way to go. It takes five generations before a breed can be called pure.

The keeper is desperate. He has formed such a bond with the gentle, amiable, beautiful shig that he will be inconsolable without her. As he stands on a stepladder to style her fleece, combing away the twigs and leaves that have caught up in it, the keeper murmurs endearments to her. He loves her in a way that it is only possible to love something that is entirely dependent on you, like a baby or a pet. In both cases it is tempting to talk to them because they seem to understand you even though they can't talk back. The keeper cannot get his arms all the way round the shig's body because she is so large, but he clasps her neck and whispers very close to her ear so he can tell her about the Cerne Abbas giant.

Scientists reporting on the genetic trials taking place around the world are very cautious about revealing the locations of the test sites because of opposition to their work from activists, and have decided to use a code rather than name the locations. Tiring of the over-familiar letters of the Greek alphabet they have used in equations since their school days, they have assigned the following symbols for each test site:

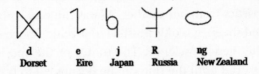

d	e	j	R	ng
Dorset	**Eire**	**Japan**	**Russia**	**New Zealand**

In Europe, transgenic celery, tobacco and sugar beet are being grown under controlled conditions, monitored, then destroyed to comply with tough licences issued by cautious EC countries. In the Republic of Ireland, a previously unknown group of activists have claimed responsibility for slashing a field of genetically altered sugar beet. In London, a group of naked protesters has climbed on the roof of advertising agency Bartle, Bogle & Hegarty to register disapproval of their work for geneticists. In Japan, people are frightened that genetically mutated vegetables will escape into the wild. In view of the growing sympathy for the havoc wreaked by environmental activists, Emphglott's project in the southwest of England is being carried out under conditions of utmost secrecy. It is only in New Zealand, a country celebrated by some for being reminiscent of England in the fifties, that people are relaxed about the changes being wrought on nature by man and are prepared to consume genetically altered vegetables.

Tired, dirty activists, their hair matted, their hands muddy, their fingernails broken from stabbing at sugar beet and wrenching it from the earth by the roots, make the ferry trip between Ireland and England. Before dispersing to tea and hot baths in their respective homes, a folded piece of paper annotated with runes is passed from hand to hand, slipped under a mohair jumper and tucked into a safe hiding place inside the waistband of an activist's second-hand combat trousers. Hands clasp and release as the ferry draws into port, taking leave of each other until summoned by the list-keeper, by mobile phone, to hit the next target.

At midnight, too late for a social visit, Clive stops for a moment by the stone birdbath in his sister's moonlit garden. His reflection, caught on the oily film of the surface of the water, is like the wicked witch in *The Wizard of Oz*. Clive, excluded from Fitzgerald's Bureau of Investigation because he is a man, and because he is irritating and selfish, is undertaking an investigation of his own.

Close to the darkened glass of her kitchen window, his fingertips smear the surface of the windowpane as he leans in among the geraniums and watches the interior of his sister's house. In the sitting room, under the bright light shed by a maroon silk, tasselled standard lamp, Mrs. Fitzgerald dozes in a high-backed armchair, her spectacles in her lap. Papers and files, telling the stories of her life and the lives of the people she is investigating, stack and fall around her feet.

Clive walks along the flowerbed that runs the length of the wall of the house until he reaches the sitting room window. He looks in at his sister but he doesn't wake her.

8

Surveillance

TONIGHT I'M KEEPING an unfaithful husband under surveillance in a singles bar in Kensington and it makes me
think about my love life, which makes me morose. If you
want to pick up a rent boy you go to the Crystal Rooms in
Leicester Square, and if you want a married man you go to
a singles bar. My job makes it difficult to meet a boyfriend
and sustain a relationship, but I'd like one anyway. I've no
idea where you find single men. I can't meet anyone at work
because the detective agency has only women working there.

It must be a perennial problem because the *Evening
Standard* often runs features with advice on where to meet
men. You're supposed to be able to find love at the supermarket. I popped into Iceland once on the way home from
the tube but the man behind me at the checkout had four
large blocks of lard and two bottles of bleach in his basket,
and kept looking at me with an urgent, hungry desire, possibly because I'd also bought bleach. I love bleach, I glug it
down the toilet and slop it into the sink as a substitute for
proper cleaning. However, I don't think it's a basis for falling in love with a man carrying so much lard in his basket.
It was pretty obvious that I wasn't going to find the right
kind of man in Iceland, anyway. It's quite rough, particularly

in Brixton, where a security man guards the meat. The one near Clapham Common tube isn't much better, even though there's a plaque claiming it was opened by Princess Anne. Why this snobbish, horsey woman ever got mixed up in opening such a place I cannot begin to imagine. I've switched from Tesco's in Brixton to Sainsbury's in Clapham as there's a better class of single man, including some minor celebrities, although I haven't had any luck with any of them yet. I think you're supposed to go to Safeway in the King's Road, with its innovative range of exotic fruits, but it's rather out of my way.

Once I went to the National Gallery. It was awash with beautiful foreign men, their eyes filled with longing. They didn't look at the paintings; their eyes swept the faces of the women there, searching for a sign. I wasn't sure what sign to give so I went home.

Now I'm sitting in a bar with lipstick and a push-up bra on, purely in the interest of blending into the crowd. No wonder I never do this. I have a suspicion that everyone else here is younger and has more stamina than me for sitting around in a smoky, masculine atmosphere surrounded by tossers talking about sport and money. I'd much rather be at home lying full length on my sofa on soft cushions in loose, shabby clothes without underwear, reading the Sunday colour supplements or watching *ER* with a large packet of peanut M&M's or a box of liqueur chocolates, the mix of alcohol and sugar crystals oozing under my tongue and dribbling down my chin. Still, you can't have everything. So here I am sitting in a bar feeling old and looking tarty and pitying the other women who seem to hope a man in a suit will want them, even though they don't really want him.

To get off with a man in one of these places you need to know the names and makes of cars and have more than a rough idea of how many people you need to make up a football team. I went to a girls' school where we played net-ball and hockey, but I think there are either eleven, twelve, or fourteen people in a football team, including the goalie. I don't suppose they'd have thirteen players as that would be unlucky. I don't really want to know. I'd rather die a lonely spinster than make concessions to the brittle new-laddishness sweeping the country by taking an interest in sport.

I've ended my 'just sex' arrangement, although it was convenient because I could ring him when I wanted to have sex and he'd come round. He always smelled of soap when he visited me. He was meticulously clean, scrubbing his whole body carefully in the shower before he visited me, shaving and dabbing himself with aftershave. Soap is very nice, but only strangers smell of soap. It's nice to wake up next to someone who smells of sex and sweat and sleep, to smell them when they come home to you before they take a shower. Maybe that's why women have office affairs, brushing next to someone at an after-work drink when he smells tired and vulnerable, his shirt smelling of sweat and just the mellow top notes of his aftershave because the astringent has faded since this morning—nothing unpleasant, but the shirt would be no good to wear tomorrow. It's an intimacy you usually only share when you live with someone and kiss them hello after work and talk to them with a gin and tonic while they have a bath and then perhaps mix their clothes up with yours to go in the washing machine while they dry themselves off.

I've been sitting at the bar sipping at an orange juice, but thinking about gin and a naked man in a bath makes me want to swish some alcohol around my mouth, so I order a Bombay Sapphire and tonic. One drink won't hurt, it might even cheer me up a bit. After two mouthfuls of the drink, which is expensive enough to be a double, the alcohol flushes through my blood and I realize that I'm miserable and I've been scowling. I totter off to the cigarette machine to get some Marlboro Lights. I gave up smoking when I was married, but I've started again since I got this job. It's a dangerous and expensive habit, but on the plus side, it's a great way to get people talking. *Have you got a light?* There's a confederacy of smokers; we're outnumbered, out of fashion, desperate for a fag. Also, I'm a bit afraid of the dark and I find it comforting to sit in my car on cold nights watching someone's house and sniffing the nicotine on my fingers.

Although we're both quite drunk by the time we leave the bar, the unfaithful husband doesn't score and nor do I.

The next night I'm sitting in the car to keep his house under surveillance. It's his night for babysitting while his wife goes to evening classes to learn Mandarin at the local sixth-form college. I don't expect him to go out anywhere, so Taron is with me, keeping me company. We tell each other stories to pass the time. We have to turn off the radio and concentrate very carefully (Taron's idea, she calls it telepathy) so that the words we say can project images into each other's mind.

Taron tells me about her husband. He's appeared in different mythologized incarnations each time she's talked about him. Sometimes he's a cartoon, square-jawed and handsome, his character served up as the sum of his features—neat, dark hair, sparkling eyes, cleanly shaven, his mouth a cupid's bow. Taron almost makes me taste the delicate, expensive scents she tells me her perky little nose always sought on his neck—freshly laundered cotton, rose and citrus in the soap he used, a plume of cigar smoke, cinnamon or burnt orange in his aftershave, the peppermint from kisses where Taron tucked her chewing gum into her cheek and she licked his skin to taste it with her tongue. (The word for taste and smell in French is the same, she told me. It isn't, I looked it up when I got home.) At other times she describes humour and quirkiness spilling out of him like liquid mercury on the science bench at school, silvery and slippery. I see a smiling, smaller, slighter, younger, quicker man with curlier hair and a more rumpled appearance. Sometimes he's kind and brave, and sometimes he's mischievous.

'We met at a fabulous party celebrating the end of the decade,' Taron says, describing herself in a too-tight, too-short dress, a shimmering, cushion-breasted beacon of sex standing near the middle of the room.

Large glittering disco balls twirling ironically from the ceiling temporarily suspended their movement, the thumping base and siren diva voices in the house tunes faltered, other people in less arresting clothes fell back as mesmerically

the

beautiful Man

walked

towards

Taron,

the Woman who was able to stop the world.

The Man, who was to become her husband, took her into his arms and started the world again.

'We met in a café and started talking because we were reading the same book,' says Taron, who can't give me the title of the book. In this version, Taron, fragile and beautiful in the artificial light of a greasy spoon caff, sits at a Formica table near the window reading a book and sipping a cup of very strong tea—or perhaps she's toying with a large fried breakfast, as thin people do. She hunches over her book concentrating, her tiny feet on the chair opposite, her legs cold in her jeans because it is an early morning in autumn, arms crossed in an effort to keep warm the perfect breasts softened by folds of her sloppily too-big, cream-coloured, casual jumper. She is Youth. An attractive young man, messy brown hair, oval face, huge, brown, intelligent eyes, smiling cupid's bow, shyly comes into the empty café, taking the seat opposite. He is Youth. He has seen her through the window and fallen in love. He mentions the book; his comment is witty, diffident and intelligent, and she also falls in love. He is the man who is to become her husband, and they warm the world with their laughter.

'Isn't he French?' I asked once, making the mistake of taking one of her stories too seriously.

'French?' She widened her eyes very, very slightly. 'He has some French heritage, yes. He looks French.'

'Torn from the pages of a magazine?'

'That's beautiful, "torn from the pages of a magazine", yeah, that's him.' She gave me the most wonderful smile, with a faraway look in her eyes as if I were the one making him up, not her. It really breaks down my defences when I'm trying to pick a fight with someone and they agree with me. I grinned at her.

'We just got married for the ceremony, we thought it would be fun. The wedding cake was a tower built of white icing with those little figures of a man and woman on the top. We never really moved in together, though, we kept our own places. He'd come and stay for a while, and when he left I'd lie in bed enjoying the peace and enjoying missing him. At first, when I was with him I was more like me than I was with anyone else. I mean, when I was with him I sparkled, I felt beautiful and exotic. I said things that were funny and cute. It was like he inspired me and I really fell in love with him. But then I found I was depending on him to make me feel like that. He even seemed to be manipulating my moods so that at other times I was withdrawn and quiet. He seemed to switch me on and off. At the end I spent more time "off" and more time lying in bed missing him.'

'So what happened to him?'

'I built a fire in the hearth at my mother's house and threw salt into it every night for seven nights. It's supposed to bring back your husband if you lose him to a rival.'

'Did it work?'

'No. It turns out he didn't leave me for anyone else.'

'Did you ever think about having a baby?'

'I pretended I had one once. A little girl. I worked as a waitress for about three months a few years ago and I told them I had a daughter. When I talked about her while I was waitressing, it was as if she were real and the only reason she wasn't there with me was because I was at work. I could imagine what she'd look like, the way she behaved, the way she would smell of the full range of Johnson's baby products after I'd bathed her. Her name was Phoebe.

'I didn't even really have to talk about her much; people

just accepted that she existed. Waitressing is the sort of work where everyone's passing through, so people do these little potted introductions about you when the new staff come in, you know, "This is Taron, she runs a club once a month, she's got a little kid called Phoebe." I miss her. Little things remind me of her. I sometimes wonder, if I'd believed in her more, whether she would have really existed. I had an abortion when I was nineteen, and talking about Phoebe made up for it a bit. I'm going to have real children one day, and I'm going to raise my daughters wearing loose shoes, maybe one or two sizes too big so that their toes bunch up slightly to grip, like delicate animals clinging to something. Then they'll look vulnerable with naked feet and men will fall in love with them and want to protect them.' Is this what she meant when she said her husband made her say cute things?

'I'd like to have children,' I confess, 'but I don't want to get pregnant and give birth. I've got a friend who's had a baby. There's a latticework of scars across her stomach where the papery skin didn't stretch quickly enough when she was pregnant. She says it looks as if someone tried to force the flesh through a chip basket. She used to lather herself with Revlon Intensive Care cream every night in vain when the marks started appearing. The rich, expensive smell makes her feel dizzy and intensely unhappy if she catches the scent on someone else. I don't want to be pregnant. I'd like to go home one night and realize I'd forgotten I already had some children. They'd all be waiting for me, lined up in matching clothes like *The Sound of Music*. I imagine running barefoot on the sand with them, their hair streaming out behind them, the same colour as mine, brightly coloured fishing nets and matching buckets and spades in their hands.'

'No dad?'

'I never see him. Perhaps he's mending the car, or whatever it is that men do. I only see the children and the fishing nets, and sometimes I'm carrying sandwiches and crisps in a raffia basket. No dad.'

'Alison, do you think you could help me find a baby?'

Well, Christ on a stick. I thought she'd forgotten about all that. I can do the research and work out where people usually leave them, but I don't think I can actually find a baby and hand it over to her mad mum. The good thing is that the chances of actually finding one have to be pretty slim.

'The chances of finding one are pretty slim,' I say, apologetically.

'My mother needs help. She's living a very lonely life, in a converted lighthouse on the Kent coast, fighting the forces of evil. Please help me.'

I'm more convinced than ever that it would be a mistake to give Taron's mother an abandoned baby if she's going to be clattering up and down steel ladders with it in a remote property miles from the rational world in Kent. Even so, Taron's pleas have touched my heart. I want to be able to keep seeing her, and I'd like to let her think that she's helping her mother in some way.

'Leave it with me. I'll do some work and find out where people leave their babies when they don't want them. I'll get back to you on it, OK?'

Chances are she'll get bored with the project after a while.

It's a relief to get home to Jeff. I call on him to check up on his progress with the advert. It's early morning, the beginning of his day, the end of mine. 'They've just vacated the last manned lighthouse in the British Isles,' he tells me when I talk about Taron and her mother. 'It was in Guernsey.'

'I was fishing for sympathy, not facts,' I say, a bit crossly.

He moves on to what he hopes will be safer ground by focusing on the women's interest areas of his life, but he ends up scaring me because he talks about the girl in the Patent Office again. She's burning with love for Jeff under her shapeless clothes. 'I think she likes me because I'm young and modern,' he says. 'She's like Audrey Hepburn in *Funny Face*. Have you seen it? She works in a bookshop before she's a model; she wears glasses and long skirts. She climbs these really high ladders to get to shelves of dusty books. It would be funny if they filed the patents like that, wouldn't it?'

'If she looks like Audrey Hepburn then she's probably anorexic. If you look closely, she's probably got a moustache. Anorexia makes them very whiskery,' I say severely. Jeff looks at me strangely. If he ever stops loving me, I'll have to start loving him to get him back. I watch him very closely for the signs.

I show Jeff a story in the paper about a German professor who has written a book on manners. He's so polite that he stands up when he hears a woman's voice on the phone.

A few days later, as the sun is unseasonably fierce for June, I arrange to meet Taron at Tooting Bec Lido to catch some rays. It's worth getting down there before the school holidays when it gets really crowded. As we pay our money and step through the turnstiles, the sight is pure English summer. You look down the length of the wide, blue pool towards a pale blue art-deco-style café with a pale blue wedding cake fountain and sundial in front of it. A blackboard in the café describes comprehensive variations on an English breakfast but, tantalizingly, these are not available after ten a.m. when the pool opens to the public. The public doesn't seem bothered and queues to buy lots of chips, crisps, cans of Coke and tea.

Tooting Bec Lido has the biggest outdoor pool in England and as a consequence the water is very cold, barely warmed by the wee of the preschool kids and their parents using it today. Everyone at the Lido smokes. Brown people sit at the edge of the pool, dangling their legs, tapping cigarette ash into the water. Most people are also tattooed—the women more extensively than the men. The women under the age of twenty-five are pregnant, eight months of swollen, stretched, smooth, hard belly in a bikini in the queue for chips. All the men have erections, including the gay ones, so their arousal can't be a response to the women's fecundity; it must be something to do with the sunshine and the fresh air.

Taron and I find ourselves a place to sit at the back of the pool behind the children's playground and the café where there's a grassy area and some trees. This place is very popular with young families, whereas single people mostly stick to the side of the pool so the water will reflect the sun and make them browner. Women picnicking near us on the grass advise their toddlers to 'tiddle' in the bushes rather than walk to the toilets conveniently sited near the pool. 'Are you going to do a poo?' they ask the children. 'If you're going to do a poo I'll put your nappy on.' As if squashing the shit against the child's skin is preferable to taking them to the toilet and teaching them to use it.

There are only same-sex groups at the Lido today, if you count the young boys with their mothers as being sexless. Most of us sit on the grass and drink lager and smoke dope while the children play on inflatable toys among the discarded plasters in the pool. There are a couple of young men near us in the trees. As they don't have children, they busy themselves playing manly games like kicking footballs and throwing Frisbees to each other. When they miss and the Frisbee plops on the ground close to the mothers, the mothers scold the young men pleasantly enough, even though they're about the same age.

As the trains thunder past, Taron and I scrutinize the other people at the Lido, speculate about their relationships and discuss their appearance. We notice a correlation between the sagging skin and drooping breasts of the women and the daring cut and shininess of their bikinis. Any young girls who aren't pregnant wear Speedo swimsuits or fifties-style bathers that hide their pubic areas. Older women wear fake snakeskin string bikinis cut to just below the pouch on their stomachs where the muscles have lost elasticity in pregnancy, silver rivers of stretch marks running up and down the skin, or in crop circle patterns around the belly button. I draw a Venn diagram on the inside front cover of D. H. Lawrence's short stories that I have brought to the Lido but I'm making no attempt to read.

Tooting Bec Lido Venn Diagram

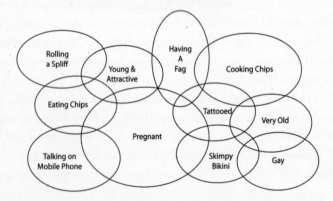

9

Taron's Mother

TARON'S MOTHER IS a very pretty woman with dark hair, looking a little like Ava Gardner in her heyday. There are no outward indications that she's a witch. She rarely leaves the house and has taken some trouble over her appearance, wearing an elegant, fitted jersey dress for her outing to the post office to buy a tax disc for her car. She's rather proud that she's never had to use stamps. In the past, if she wanted to get a message to someone anywhere in the world, she would send a psychic postcard by thinking very hard about a message she wanted to convey. Because of the amount of effort it takes to send information in this way, and the varying lack of skill in the receiver in decoding it, she could only really send something of postcard length, and often with a similarly superficial tone. Taron's mother found it so draining, she's glad she's mostly been able to replace this method of communication with Internet, e-mail and mobile phones. She doesn't even have to use psychic phenomena to check her bank balance anymore since the introduction of twenty-four-hour telephone banking, which has freed up a tremendous amount of her energy.

As she returns from the post office she gets a premonition. She takes out her mobile phone and tries to get through on it, but reaches only her daughter's voicemail.

She stands very still in the middle of the high street, closes her eyes, touches one hand to her temple. Because of the nature of the message she feels she must send, it comes across as something darker than a psychic postcard. *DANGER*, she thinks. *DANGER. DANGER.* Unlike e-mail, she cannot put a receipt on the message, so she cannot be sure Taron has received it.

10

The Raid

IT'S A THURSDAY in July. It's been a long day and I feel tired and miserable as I finish work. I found a poem taped to a tube of Smarties when I got up this morning:

Melting
Lips smudge Smartie colours
Tongue tastes mixed-up flavours
As chocolate melts
Inside your mouth
Clapping hands believe in fairies
I believe in the warm place
Where chocolate melts
Inside your mouth

I wonder if this is an obscure blow job allusion and it puts me in a bad mood for the rest of the day. Thursday. It's not quite the end of the week but it's near enough to celebrate if anyone else is up for it. Taron calls me to meet up with her for a drink at about seven p.m. I feel that I'm missing her as soon as I hear her voice, a light breeze on the phone line to where I'm working undercover in an office, combustingly hot in a pair of thick tights. Sheer tights, while elegant and cooler to wear, are three pounds a pair and you're guaranteed to put your thumb through them before the end of the first day you wear them. Thick tights—six pounds a pair, wear 'em and wash 'em and wear 'em again until bobbles appear on the legs—heat the core of your body until you feel your head will explode. The government should issue warnings in the same way they do for young people taking drugs at raves (drink half a litre of water an hour, take plenty of breaks, be safe). I once fainted on a shuttle flight from Glasgow to London because the tights I was wearing were too thick. None of the other passengers would talk to me because I had made a show of myself.

The reason I'm so miserable now is that I shouldn't have to be thinking about tights at all. I took the detective job because I didn't want to prostrate myself on the altar of commerce, and yet here I am anyway, albeit as a spy in the house of love, which today is the office of Jones, Kibble, Parsnip in the city of London where some bloke may be shagging his secretary. I know retro is fashionable but shagging your secretary is just too tiresomely seventies. I'm working here as a temp in a long wrapover skirt and a translucent white blouse so you can see the rather pointy bra I'm wearing. And the bloody tights. And some specs. This is the universal uniform for temps, I hope. The girls in the office seem convinced by my disguise. They tell me shag-bloke's a rat and he goes at it hammer and tongs with his secretary in the toilets at work. I feel miserable as I leave the office tonight, and suddenly Taron represents a kind of logic and stability in this crazy world. At any rate, even though her head is filled with nonsense, I think the only person she has ever deceived is herself.

She tells me the name of a bar we can meet in. It's near where she lives. When we meet, I'm struck by how pretty she is, how funny, how gentle, how sane. She makes me take off the tights in the toilets of the bar and puts a glass ring on my finger, which she says will ward off the bad vibes I soaked up in the office today. 'I've been getting a bad feeling all day,' she says. We aren't in a bar, really, it's a pub. For some reason I think this harmless pretention is charming.

We drink two beers very quickly. I'm not sure whether it's the alcohol, the tights-off relief, the magic ring, or Taron herself, but I gradually re-humanize and cheer up. Now I'm marginally pissed, cheered up, guilty for being miserable earlier, and pretty much in the mood for whatever the evening has in store.

I confess that the job is getting me down. 'Come away with me,' says Taron. 'Come away with me and help me find a baby.' It would almost be an attractive idea if it weren't so mad. After I finish up tomorrow by taking a few shots of the toilet sex (let's hope they do it in the girls' toilets and not the boys'; I don't fancy sloshing around in the urinals setting up my hidden camera) I don't really have much work on for the next week or so. It would be nice to let Taron garland me with good-vibes jewellery and drive around the country collecting babies to get in her mother's good books. I smile at Taron in what I hope is an impish and affectionate way. I'd quite like to drive around with her forever and never have to do another day's work again.

She puts her little hand on mine and leans forward. 'Come on,' she says, 'let's go home.' I feel that I'm really happy and maybe even the job isn't so bad at all and I should just knuckle down and get on with it so long as I can spend some of my time with Taron. We collect our things and leave the pub. I touch her hand then I turn, wondering how far it is to Taron's place and if I should have a wee before we go. Suddenly there is an incident. Everything happens very quickly and we don't react at all, we just gawp. Some guy, brushing past, has taken Taron's bag. I'd been holding it for her. He has only had to pull it gently from my hands because I didn't know what was happening. You couldn't say I'd been mugged, exactly, because there was no violence. 'Hey,' calls Taron to the thief, but she's looking at me in case I have any ideas. I don't. The guy is already out of sight, running like the clappers and now in possession of Taron's bag containing her keys, money, makeup, address book, mobile phone, and my tights. The bag is pretty heavy because she carries horseshoes clanking at the bottom of it so she can leave them around the place for good luck, as a way of improving the world. Let's hope they do the robber more good than they've done us tonight. We didn't see him at all—couldn't describe his age, his colour. I've never been the victim of robbery or violence and I've always wondered how I'd react—whether I'd fight or freeze. I didn't expect to be so insipid, standing sheepishly about. 'Oh well,' we say, still looking at each other.

'Let's go back to your place,' said Taron. 'We can call the police from there.' She probably has a little stash of drugs at home and doesn't want to call the police from her flat. Like they could care. I feel quite tired again but Taron looks shaky and I should look after her, so I take her home.

I know something is wrong as soon as we go inside the door. Everything has been disturbed. Someone has systematically been through all my things. I carefully assess the damage. The computer has gone, my files have been rifled, the film removed from my camera. I feel suddenly very upset and sick. I realize that I've been checking my things so intently I've been oblivious to Taron. I find her sitting on the sofa weeping very quietly. This makes me feel more miserable, and I give her a sisterly cuddle before going to make some tea. 'It's like *The X Files,*' she says. I'd laugh to cheer her up but I agree, in a way. Someone has looked through all the information I have in my house and either found what they wanted (who knows?) or will come back for more. It wasn't an ordinary burglary. My TV and my wedding ring are still in the house. Perhaps one of the unfaithful husbands I've been following is a secret agent (the south London area I cover is a handy commuter distance for the new MI6 building on the Vauxhall Bridge) and I've stumbled onto something BIG. Well, that's the way it would work if this were a movie.

Taron and I spend some time discussing who would play us in the film. We're not sure about Julia Roberts—isn't she past her heyday?—so in the end I go for Kristin Scott Thomas. Taron wastes some time trying to remember the name of the beautiful actress in the *Red Lantern* (it's Gong Li, but I have to look it up later) and we bicker over whether or not the burglar in the film, in the form of Ewan McGregor, would still be hiding in my house and would fall in love with us, and if so which one he would prefer. Perhaps he would shoot one of us by mistake and the doctor looking after us would be George Clooney and one of us could have him. I always talk bollocks when I'm nervous.

'What about John Cusack?'

'What about him?'

'Well, I quite fancy him.'

'Well, I quite fancy Robert Downey Jr., but what's that got to do with anything, Alison?'

'I don't think you'd want Robert Downey Jr. around, he drove through Hollywood stark naked with a gun in his car.'

'You're completely missing the point. He's not ever going to be around. He lives in America and I live in England.' Also, he's a movie star and she's unemployed.

As soon as we stop talking, I feel quite frightened again. Perhaps the people at MI6 will imprison us under the Thames, our screams masked by the bilgey waters above us and by the music from the dodgy nightclubs in the surrounding Vauxhall area. How long would they torture us before they realized we truly didn't know anything and weren't just being brave? How many of Taron's stories would they believe before they killed us for being mad liars?

Luckily, I have some chocolate-covered Rich Tea biscuits, so we have half a packet of those each with our tea and talk about the burglary. We call it 'The Raid.'

'OK,' says Taron, who likes to think she has a keen analytical mind, 'OK, so what are the motives for The Raid? Either Ewan McGregor is working alone, he's a disgruntled, unfaithful husband—'

'—or been hired by one.'

'—or been hired by one. In which case he's got what he wanted and he'll leave you alone. Or he's a spy and he has the backup of a huge, powerful organization and he won't stop till he's crushed you.'

'Right. Well, talking things through with you has made me feel much better. I think it could be linked to a new project I'm working on; I'm investigating a company with a dodgy animal rights record that's making a big investment in a secret project in the southwest of England.'

I feel powerless and unhappy. We decide not to call the police in case the break-in does have something to do with Emphglott. Then we realize we have to call them so I can claim on the insurance for the computer. We call them and they're sympathetic but say there isn't anything they can do to help. We don't mention *The X Files*, MI6 or Taron's drugs, so they don't come round. 'In the film,' I say to Taron, 'we might get off with one of the policemen.'

'No.' She's tired and quite snappy by now. 'Because we're anti-establishment and we don't do it with anyone who is the establishment, except George Clooney, who isn't counted because although he's played a doctor he's not the marrying kind. The sort of people who play policemen are Clint Eastwood or the Bridges brothers, and you don't want one of them.' She's right, of course, I'm not with it at all. We decide to call it a night and she goes home. Before she leaves, she advises me to put cactuses in each window to guard the house.

As I brush my teeth, I check the horseshoe she left in my bathroom cabinet on her first visit. Still there, exuding its too-weak magic. Perhaps I'm being unfair and we owe the fact we weren't hurt in either of the attacks to Taron's lucky charms, the way Sleeping Beauty owed her long sleep to the last fairy at the christening.

I lie awake, unable to sleep even though I lie very still and try to retreat inside myself, visualizing somewhere calm and relaxing. I keep getting put off by the picture of the Virgin Mary I bought recently to go with my Jesus. Mary is about the same age as Jesus the way the artist has drawn them, so they look more like lovers than mother and son. Her face, with its aching sympathy and gentle understanding, has begun to irk me because for some reason I think of the patent office girl whenever I look at her. There they are, side by side on my wall, Jesus and the patent office girl, all loving and suffering. Even when my eyes are closed, theirs are open, eternally vigilant. As I retreat inside myself I find them there with their blazing hearts and halos.

I awake with a start in the middle of the night, heart jumping because of some noise inside or outside the house, too frightened to get out of bed for a pee in case someone has broken in again or didn't ever leave and a murderer is waiting in the shadows. Darkness brings back my childhood fears and makes me irrational. A murderer wouldn't be playing a waiting game, triggered into harming me by my visit to the toilet. Only monsters behave like that. It isn't until dawn comes that I work this out, and so I pass an uncomfortable bladderful few hours waiting for the darkness to ease.

11

The Psychic Postcard

THE NEXT DAY, a little too late to be of any use, the psychic postman writes a message on one of a stack of cheap postcards with views of London he carries with him and he pushes it through Alison's letterbox. DANGER, he writes, BEWARE. Taron's mother has taken the precaution of communicating through him in case Taron was listening to loud music yesterday, mistook the words her mother was sending for a subliminal message from the musicians, and ignored them.

As no other post office employees have been involved, the psychic postman does not put a stamp on the postcard before putting it in through Alison's front door. He doesn't regularly deprive his employers of revenue in this way; nevertheless it is not something they would encourage if they knew about it.

Taron's handbag presents an interesting puzzle for the people who wanted it stolen. The man they engaged for the task was a poor choice. He was supposed to take Alison's bag but he took Taron's, believing it to be close enough. It isn't.

Two men sort through the contents of Taron's bag, exchanging grunting noises that pass for conversation as they work. Perhaps they have sinus problems or perhaps, after all, their past lives in the Metropolitan Police have injected an oink into their vocabulary. Their fingers pass over the usual women's junk things that they can reasonably ignore, like peppermint lip gloss and chewing gum and very small screwed-up pieces of paper. It's a myth that women's handbags are always full of tampons. There's no point in carrying them around unless you need them because if you leave them at the bottom of your handbag they get scuffed, covered in lipstick and pen, and finally unravel so that they are useless. Taron carries thirty-five or forty keys with her. She believes that keys bring extreme good fortune to the carrier, but only if they don't fit any of the doors in that person's house. It's as well that Bird's men recognize that patience is a virtue, because they will need it in sifting through Taron's bag for clues. The address book, at least, will be of use, most of the entries adorned with symbols that look as if they could bear decoding. The boys in Waterloo can input all the names and addresses to cross-refer with the others on the database. Perhaps it's worth having someone pay one or two of the people in the address book a visit to find out whether they know if Alison Temple is onto something.

Flower sits handsomely at his desk and skims through the weekly updates on current activity in his agency. For security reasons, agents usually dial in remotely to a computer system for lists of people they've been assigned to investigate. Managers brief them face-to-face on the objectives of surveillance projects without knowing the names of individuals who are being targeted. Operatives submit weekly or even daily reports direct to Flower. Sometimes their activities yield nothing, usually because the integrity of the data cannot be relied on. Bird, still searching in vain for information about the genetic experimentation sites being targeted by terrorists, passed him some names for investigation, but so far the leads have been useless. Flower reads through the latest report with a sigh.

Date: June 27th
Objective: Determine subject's terrorist status and
               access to sensitive information.

Gained entry to subject's flat. Evidence suggests that the place had previously been searched by amateur—clothing tipped out of drawers & lying in piles on floor.

Subject does not appear to have been in residence for many days—dirty cups in sink, no food in fridge, no toilet paper. May have disappeared in hurry—to undertake terrorist activity?

Suspect is male and appears to live alone but there are quantities of female apparel and maquillage in flat. Pantomime horse costume in wardrobe.

No data found on premises. No evidence of intelligence gathering. No evidence of links to subversive organizations.

Recommend further action.

They always recommend further action. It keeps them busy and in gainful employment. There are three main steps the operatives follow in obtaining information about each subject: step 1) suss 'em out, step 2) shake 'em down, step 3) rough 'em up. They rarely get to stage 3 but they always recommend it. Even though he's handsome and even though he isn't the top man in his organization, Flower has been in the business long enough to recognize a report without information of any value. He recommends no further action. It's the fifth or sixth useless lead in as many days. He hopes Bird draws a similar conclusion. There's a saying in the corporate world that like recruits like, and Bird has recruited men in his image, dangerous men. Someone's going to get hurt one of these days.

12

The Dogs

'ALISON.' Taron is on the phone. She says my name urgently, breathily, so I know she's upset. She pauses so I can take it in. Should have been an actress. 'Something really strange is happening. Something's happening to all my friends. Alison?'

'What time is it?' I'm asleep and disoriented. I've been having a dream about the newspaper report Jeff and I read today, about two dogs who dialled 999 while their owner was out. The emergency services suspected their frantic, panting breath on the phone was a nuisance call, but when they investigated they found the dogs had ransacked their own home. A police spokesman was quoted as saying that it was quite possible that one or both of the dogs had dialled the numbers using their paws or their noses. Jeff and I disagreed, thinking it unlikely the dogs would have felt guilty and wanted to give themselves up. The only explanation that worked for us was that the dogs had fallen out and one of them had dobbed the other in to the coppers.

'It's just after midnight. Wake up, Alison. Something really strange is happening. You know Aani's flat was turned over but they didn't take anything? Well, the same thing's happened to more of my friends but GET THIS—it's happening in alphabetical order, exactly the order I've listed them in my address book. Aani, Aaron, Alexis.'

Who'd alphabetize by first names except Taron? At first, I'm struck more by how irritating this is than by the danger to her friends. Then I start to see the connection she's making—that whoever went through my flat, the same person stole her bag with the address book in it, is targeting everyone in it, painstakingly working their way through the transvestites, performance artistes, drug dealers and club kids listed in her book.

'I think we're all in danger. This has got to be something to do with your work. I bet whoever stole that bag thought it belonged to you.'

'Have you got a copy of your address book so we can contact your friends?'

'No.'

Her friends are the sort of people who don't just externalize their feelings, they externalize all aspects of their lives, including their domestic arrangements. They'll have an untidy cupboard-sized room they call home but I'd be more inclined to call a dressing-up box, spilling with wings and false eyelashes, drugs, cheap alcohol and chewing gum. They eat out, sleep over and bathe with friends, where possible. They only return to change and check the answer machine. It's a surprise any of them can even tell someone's broken in and been through their things.

'What about in old diaries or on your mobile phone?'

'They've got the moby, it was in my bag. Wait. I've just thought of something. I have got a copy of my address book but it's in my bank vault.'

'You've got a bank vault?'

'It's in Barclays Bank in Piccadilly, do you want to come and see tomorrow?'

13

Alvin

LIKE MOST FAT people's hands, Alvin's hands are beautifully kept. Children playing hide-and-seek think that if they can't see you, you can't see them. As fat people only see their own hands for most of the day, do they think that's all the rest of the world sees and so let their bodies go to rack and ruin?

Alvin is on the point of leaving his flat. He turns off the TV with the remote control, glancing down at his hands as he does so. They're the last clear, normal image he has before the horror begins.

He looks up to see two men in his flat. They, like he, are fashionably dressed in black. There the resemblance ends. Alvin is one of those straight men who has cultivated the art of camp as a way of being entertaining. His mixture of wit and wobble is highly valued on the party circuit and makes him popular with women looking for a nonthreatening, nonsexual relationship. The men in his flat are villainous thugs. They advertise the fact with their haircuts and scratchy stubble. Also, one carries a hunting knife unsheathed in front of him.

Alvin focuses on the weapon there in the man's hands, dangerous, sharp. To avoid antagonizing them, he doesn't look directly into the men's faces. They haven't moved or spoken since he first saw them. Absurdly, Alvin wonders whether they've seen him. Perhaps if he stays really still…?

'We know you are an associate of Alison Temple,' says the man, menacingly. 'What do you have to say to that?' Alvin is relieved. He's never heard of her. Obviously this can all be sorted out. He's almost calm. He acts the way he would in a restaurant when he sees they have put one too many bottles of wine on the bill. It's probably just as well Alvin doesn't get cocky and also that he's straight. So many overweight homosexuals have come to believe they are imbued with the spirit of Oscar Wilde. There is no place for epigrams in a situation like this.

'Oh, I think there's been a mistake.'

'There is no mistake,' says the menacing man. 'Do you see this knife? What do you think I could do with this?' Alvin considers the response carefully. He does not want to suggest something so ghastly or original that they're inspired to carry it out. But, in case they are bullying psychopaths waiting for him to break the rules of a game only they understand, he wants to appear to be entering into the spirit of things. 'Cut my hair' sounds a little too tame, even though it has many resonances through history as a way of curtailing power or bringing shame. Alvin eventually settles on 'You might stab me' as being fairly noncommittal but respectful of the power of the blade.

'What else?' The restraint of his maybe-torturers is menacing. So far they have done nothing violent, and yet the air in the flat is oppressive with threat.

Alvin is silent. Power always makes people act the same way—sneering, knowing, over-reliant on rhetorical questions, wanting you to acknowledge the power. The lack of elegance in their manner would offend him if he weren't genuinely frightened. He thinks of an article he read in the paper where they asked celebrities what they would do if they saw a fight outside a pub. Some said they'd try to break it up, others said they'd telephone the police. Performance artist Leigh Bowery said he'd judge the fight on artistic merit.

'Don't you think we know how to make you squeal? How do you think we get people to talk?'

In spite of himself, Alvin visualizes some of the options. He thinks they might make men talk by stabbing them in the balls, jabbing them in the eye or heating the blade of the knife over a naked flame and searing their shrinking flesh.

He'd like to have an easy, clubbable way about him. *Come on, fellas. What's this all about?* One of Alvin's strengths is that he knows his own limitations: 'I'll tell you whatever you want to know. What do you want to know? Perhaps I do know this Alison but under another name?'

'Let me make this easy, Alvin.' It's the first time he's said the name and Alvin's stomach turns over. The man moves the knife a little, deliberately, to draw attention to its power. 'I'll tell you what we know and you tell me what you know. We know Alison has connections with eco-activists. We know you know her. We'd like to know how much she knows about these criminals. And we'd like to be sure she knows the risks involved.'

'I don't know anything. No activism. No eco-warring. I don't know any Alisons. I belong to the world of entertainment.'

'Entertain us, then,' says the knife man. His accomplice moves quickly, kicking Alvin very hard and punching him in the head as he goes down. His fist connects with teeth and makes a cracking sound. Alvin, gym-muscular under the fat, is fit enough to remain conscious while the shit is kicked out of him. He curls up to protect his belly and his balls and puts his hands over his head. The silent man kicks his arse, his kidneys and his hands where they grip his head. Alvin feels nauseous and afraid. He didn't ask, and perhaps they wouldn't have told him, but he has no idea who they are. They could be anyone. They could kick him until he dies. When he thinks they won't stop, they stop. 'We'll be watching you. Tell Alison,' says the menacing man.

14

The Bank

I MEET TARON at the bank. It's very grand and old, situated just along from the Ritz. It has a domed roof and wrought iron gates with a leaf motif picked out in gold. There is a mosaic in the floor and the counter is cool enough to the touch to be real marble. Despite the splendour of their surroundings, the staff here, as in every other branch of Barclays, are kitted out in aquamarine suits as if they are flying on a charter aircraft. Taron and I tiptoe down a marble staircase grand enough to suggest we will find more staff dancing in aquamarine formation below us, but instead of a ballroom we reach the bank where Taron keeps her treasures.

She's twitchy with pleasure as she shows me what is inside. 'I feel like Audrey Hepburn in *Breakfast at Tiffany's* when I come here,' she explains, raking her fingers through handfuls of costume jewellery. It's like being a guest at a dinner party at which you have to say goodnight to the host's precocious daughter and you're trapped there playing with her in her bedroom until someone notices you're missing and comes to find you.

'Here's a pearl in an oyster,' she says, holding up a clear container the size of a tin of tuna. Inside there's some blurry water swirling about and I can make out an oyster. The writing on the container announces the oyster contains a freshwater pearl from San Francisco. 'Did you ever see *Singin' in the Rain*, and there's that scene where they always order oysters because they want to find a pearl and then they find one? My husband gave me this because he knows I like the film.' I wonder whether there is a best-before date on the lid and squint to try and see. It strikes me as a bit unhygienic.

'Is this real?' I ask about the jewellery.

'I pretend it is.'

'What's this?' I have found a piece of parchment, yellowed and curling. It is very mysterious. Someone has written on it in ink, in spidery writing:

Del *.*

'My mother gave it to me. She said the symbols are very powerful. One day I may have to use it. When the time comes, I will know.'

'D E L star dot star?'

'Yes.'

'Is it like a spell?'

'Yes.'

The address book is there and when she holds it, Taron's face changes as if she's in love. 'This was my whole life, once,' she says softly.

As she flicks through the pages, I can see she's used symbols against most of the names. 'What are those?'

'They're runes. This one means *f,* so if I put it next to someone's name it means fun or freaky. This is *d* for don't. Like when they're dead from the neck up. This is *h* for horny. This means *g* for gagging.' There are lots of *g* symbols. 'This is *e*, and this is *t* for tranny. Trannies are really popular at straight parties because the straights think they're in for a really wild night if they see a few men wandering around in big hair and sticky lipstick…This one is *r* for rocking.'

'What's *e* for?'

'*E* is for E. It means they can usually sort you out at a party if you give them a call first.'

Our trip to the bank is a pleasant interlude, but when we come home and start to phone people to warn them that they and we are in danger, we get frightened again and start to feel tense. What if someone breaks in while one of Taron's friends is at home? Would they tie them up or kill them? What happens when they don't find anything—will they come back for us when we're at home?

The phone calls follow the same pattern. 'Hi, it's Taron. How're you doing? Great. Great. Chat, chat. Listen, some guy stole my bag and he's bothering my friends and me. Sorry about this but he's got my address book. Watch out for yourself, OK? Just in case. Let's catch up, soon. Take care.' Taron doesn't want to go into too much detail because she doesn't want people thinking she's bringing bad shit into their lives. On the other hand, it's only fair to warn them.

One call is dramatically different.

'Hi, it's Taron. How're you doing?'

'Taron. Darling. Long time no hear. I'm doing shit. I'm terrible.'

'What? You sound very muffled, it must be a bad reception on your mobile. What's the matter, babe?'

'No, I just sound muffled because my mouth's all swollen. I got beaten up.'

'No, that's terrible. What happened?'

'Two men were in the flat. It was unreal. Very unpleasant. They were like James Bond baddies. Dressed in black from head to toe and carrying weapons. I didn't know whether to run for cover or ask for the name of their tailor.'

'Alvin, no. How horrible. What did they want? Why pick on you?'

'Oh well, that was the odd thing. They kept asking about some woman I didn't know. When I couldn't tell them anything, they kicked forty shades of fuck out of me. I kept hoping they wouldn't puncture anything because I didn't want to decorate my very tasteful brand new pale rug with my own leaking bodily fluids.'

'Alvin. And did they? Puncture anything?'

'No, they bruised me terribly. I've still got a map of Asia Minor on my left buttock. They broke some of my teeth, too. Three years of cosmetic dentistry fallen down through the cracks in my stripped floorboards.'

'I'm really sorry. You sound really bad. I'll think about you. I'll send some good vibes down the line. Oh. By the way, who was the woman?'

'There was no woman, sweetheart. Just the Men in Black.'

'No, the woman they were asking you about.'

'Oh, God. Well that's unreal, too. It made me think of hammy old Roger Moore. Templar, I think. You know, like that series in the sixties, *The Saint*. His name was Simon Templar. Did you ever see it?'

'Didn't they tell you her first name?'

'Alison. Alison Templar. 'Tell Alison,' they said. I was in no position to argue, curled up on the floor with my bits between my legs and my hands over my ears. Can you believe it, Taron? They were kicking me in the knackers and I had my hands over my ears. I'm too frightened to go home. Well, you know me. I'm a lover not a fighter.'

'Like Michael Jackson.'

'Yes. I'm staying with Jane Memory. Do you know her? She writes bits and pieces for the style mags. She might do something on my suffering. We must catch up. Give me a call.'

'Yes, we must catch up. Take care.'

Taron puts the phone down and turns to me. 'Alison, let's get out of London.'

'I have to work.'

'You heard what happened to Alvin. We don't want to risk something like this. It's a warning. Take a holiday. If you're worried about doing some work, you can help me find a baby.'

'Taron, you'll never find one.'

'Help me look, though.'

'I suppose it's a good idea to get away and think for a while. We can put things in perspective. What do we have to do before we go?' I start listing things, to make me feel organized and professional. 'I'll have to speak to Mrs. Fitzgerald and let her know what's going on. I'll have to tell Jeff…' That's it really. They are the only important people in my life, apart from Taron.

'I'm not gonna say anything to my mother yet, until we have some good news. I'll go back to my place and call a few more people and pack. Pick me up tomorrow morning?'

'Where shall we go?'

'As it's a holiday we should go to the seaside, but somewhere we're likely to find a baby.'

I've been checking the news reports and there are plenty of babies found in and around London, in hospitals, in dustbins, outside newsagents. Someone left one in the ladies' toilet at Heathrow recently. This doesn't really get us out of London, and anyway Taron wants us to target the coast. I plan to head south towards the warmth, and finally I decide on Weymouth as it looks as if it's on the end of a fairly straight road from London. Project Brown Dog's 'unethical activity' is in that area so maybe I can poke around. Prince Andrew was once stationed nearby at Portland naval base; perhaps we'll run into him in a nuclear submarine. Taron has something of the look of Koo Stark back in the days when she had forsaken a modelling career to step out with Prince Andrew, so maybe she'll land herself a royal now he's single again.

I walk downstairs to tell Jeff we're going away. 'Why' by Annie Lennox is on the CD player. He's kneeling on the floor making a mosaic surround for a mirror. It's one of the things he does for money until he cracks it with inventing.

'Do you know what a yabbie is?' he asks.

'No.'

'There's something I saw in the paper. I meant to keep it for you. Yabbies are a type of freshwater crayfish they only get in Australia. Geneticists in Warrnambool University in Victoria have bred a super yabbie. They'll grow faster to larger sizes in brighter colours, and they'll breed more. It made me think of that picture you keep in your wallet.'

'Why would they want them to be brighter? I shouldn't have thought they worried about aesthetics. Perhaps it's just a by-product. I came down to tell you I'm going away with Taron tomorrow.'

'Why?'

As the chorus builds on the song he's listening to, it seems as though Annie Lennox is asking the same question: 'Why?'

'We need a bit of a holiday after The Raid.'

'No, I mean why with Taron?'

'I like her. I know she can be a bit weird sometimes. I can never believe anything she says, she makes it up as she goes along. It doesn't matter. I find it quite difficult to trust anyone anyway after I caught my husband cheating on me, so I might as well be friends with someone with a fairly relaxed grip on the trust. She's a lot of fun, though. She's always up for it.' Jeff is quiet, still working. 'I didn't realize how much time I spent on my own until I started seeing her. I wasn't lonely, exactly. I spent a lot of time on my own, though. I've got you, of course. I like spending time with you, too. Thanks for telling me about the yabbie thing. That's funny. I'll call you while we're away. I'll miss you.'

'Yeah, I'll miss you, too. Take care.' He's still bending over the mosaic. Annie Lennox is still playing on the CD player. The light is quite bad so he's probably straining his eyes. Perhaps I should buy him a lamp while we're away.

I scuttle back upstairs and call Mrs. Fitzgerald's voice-mail to tell her we're going away tomorrow. Then I go to bed and fall asleep trying to work out whether Prince Andrew is counted as part of the establishment Taron says we're against or whether he's exempt because of his wealth and privilege. I dream that I take a lamp down to Jeff to help him work on the mosaic and when I look closely at the green, gold and copper squares he's cemented to the circular frame, I see the mosaic is actually made up of an interlocking pattern of exquisitely coloured super yabbies.

15

The Drive

I MAKE JEFF a cup of tea so I can take it downstairs and talk
to him about watering my garden while I'm away. I forgot to
mention it in the midst of all my confused stutterings about
Taron last night. My bare feet slide over a piece of paper.

Dust

Dust your citrus spangled love
and make me shine with it
Catch the sun in lemon drops of love
Make you mine with it

Dust will fall from the moon
and cover my heart
Before I consider leaving you
I love you

Dust my heart with sugar
Melt me
I'm syrup
I can taste lemon on your mouth
When I kiss you

Your love for me
Is like dust
Fine and light

Dust your citrus spangled love
and turn my tears to stars
I love you
But you know that anyway

Pale sunshine in the morning
When I leave your house
Without you
Blurs lemon patches on the clouds

I've seen sand that colour
On a beach
Very far away from here

I'd like to go away with you
To a place
Where the sea catches stars at night

Dust your citrus spangled love
My tears are stars
I can't go with you
But you know that anyway

I take the poem back into my house and put it with the others. Then I take it out and read it again, sipping from Jeff's cup of tea, which I still have in my hand. I don't take sugar in my tea but he has two. I enjoy the sweetness for a change. The poem makes me feel very sad. I rub the side of the teacup against my bosom to remove any germs and walk back downstairs again to find him. I walk straight into the flat as I always do. I never worry that I will disturb him, that he will be naked or fucking someone or in a bad mood. I always expect to find him alone and amenable, inventing things that I secretly find amusing. It's as if he doesn't exist except when I'm there and then only in a role that suits me. I know that this is egocentric and therefore a personality flaw.

Jeff is rubbing his pyjama trouser legs nervously when I go in but he accepts the half-measure cup of tea gratefully enough. I had decided to talk to him about the poetry but he's bare-chested, and as he isn't wearing his trademark grey T-shirt I find myself commenting on this instead. 'Well, you have lovely muscles on your arms, and no hair on your chest. That's nice,' I say. Perhaps Jeff was expecting me to dust him with my citrus spangled love, but my comments are so inane that he's jolted with surprise and the moment to exchange further confidences passes.

'Come and have some breakfast.' He has no choice but to follow me miserably upstairs as I take him by the hand and lead him to my kitchen. I'd like to make him bacon and eggs but I have neither, so I get hold of some of the porridge that I keep in the cupboard to treat him on special occasions. It's making him unhappy to see that I'm making such an effort. I line up maple syrup, golden syrup and condensed milk on the table in front of him with a flourish of schadenfreude. You always hurt the one you love. Except that I don't love him. I put plenty of milk in the porridge so it will be creamy. Well, I always have so much milk around now that I get it delivered because I only really need it for tea and coffee. I wonder whether to make him a strawberry milkshake but remember that I have no strawberry flavouring, no strawberries and no ice cream, so it would be a bit plain. Taron says that milk is the only thing guaranteed to put out fires caused by lightning but Jeff and I have yet to find an opportunity to test this information.

I soothe him by reading from the local newspaper: 'A pit containing seventy poisonous vipers has been uncovered in a garden in Streatham. Police are trying to determine whether the snakes were being bred for sale or kept as pets.'

I put my hand on his shoulder and kiss him very lightly near his mouth before he takes the stairs back to his basement to invent something else.

It's still early when I collect Taron in the car (*honk, honk*) so we can set off on our adventure. One of the things I like about Taron is that every time I see her she does something that astonishes me. I cannot get over the fact that she has packed a set of elegant luggage you would associate with a post-war cruise. The luggage is beautiful, the material stiff enough for me to knock on it and make a *tok-tok* sound, which I do. There is even a hatbox, although I don't really think it's suitable for our journey.

Taron says she wouldn't want Prince Andrew under any circumstances because he's dorky and fat. 'Don't you know that rock stars are the new royalty and comedians are the new rock stars? Don't you read *GQ* magazine?'

'What about film stars?'

'Same as always, they're really cool and everybody wants one.'

We stop off for petrol and sweets before we get onto the motorway. I buy two large packets of liquorice allsorts and a packet of milk bottles, which are chewy white sweets covered in a fine white powder. Our snack selection is completed by packs of Wagon Wheels, Jaffa Cakes and Walkers crisps. When I first learned to drive and I bought petrol, I went to great lengths to trickle the final drops into the petrol tank so it cost a round amount of money like ten pounds. Now I try and spend £19.87 or £20.04 or some other amount that I hope will disturb the cashier's sense of neatness and uniformity. I'm bluffing him, hoping he'll think I cannot control the petrol trigger properly because I'm not a man.

It takes a while to get out of London but soon the houses and offices roll back and we see the countryside. I do the driving. Taron doesn't drive following an incident she's reluctant to discuss in which she captured a black cat and rode around with the intention of releasing it in front of some unhappy people to bring them luck. The cat leapt onto her shoulders and caused her to lose control of the car, and she's since lost her nerve about driving.

Taron's small, squarish feet are resting on the glove compartment. She told me once that she bites her toenails but they look neat enough to me, painted with silver nail varnish. Occasionally she smokes a cigarette. The smell as she first lights each one is very sweet as the tobacco heats up, a comforting smell like dogs paws when they wake up from a long sleep indoors. It reminds me of car journeys when I was a child and makes me feel nostalgic. I grab handfuls of milk bottle sweets from the bag on her lap and chew them as we drive. The dust gets on my black trousers and when I try to brush it away, I seem to drive it further into the grain of the fabric. We're very happy, lost in our individual thoughts. We're playing easy listening music, love songs that make me think of my husband for the first time in years. I've talked to Taron about what he was like but I haven't really thought about the way I felt when I was in love with him.

If I think too much about him I could fall in love with him again, so instead of thinking about him as someone real, alive and difficult to pin down as a slippery silverfish, I've objectified him and trapped him in The Story of the Unfaithful Husband. In the story I don't have to explain why I loved him, only why I left him. The trouble is that he didn't change any of the reasons I had to love him, only added some reasons to hate him. I miss his arms around me. Or any man's arms, in fact. I wish I'd cuddled Jeff this morning before I left him. He must be lonely. I think I'll upgrade our relationship to include some neighbourly hugs when I get back home. Smoking makes me feel guilty and the guilt makes me feel melancholy. I've just finished one of Taron's cigarettes and perhaps it's the melancholy that makes me realize how much I would miss Jeff if he found himself a proper girlfriend and started loving her instead. The only emotion I'm afraid of is regret. If I have time while I'm away, I'll write him a poem to let him know I care and keep him interested.

The next song that plays on the CD player in the car is 'You'll Never Know' by Hi Gloss. We join in, surer of the chorus than the verse—but still investing the words with meaning as we sing along.

Taron and I don't like the pincushion liquorice allsorts sweets with the aniseed jelly in them, so we leave them in the bottom of the packet. We like the coloured sandwich ones and the plain liquorice. The round orange or pink coconut wheels with liquorice in the middle are very pretty but they're not our favourites. 'How hungry would you have to be before you ate one of the bobbly jelly ones?' asks Taron.

'I don't think they're supposed to satisfy hunger.'

'Well, how desperate to eat something sweet?'

'It'd have to be in the middle of the night somewhere on a stakeout.'

'Like in a marsh in a makeshift hide watching ducks?'

'I was thinking more about being in a car and watching a suspect.'

'I'd eat them for a dare.'

'Go on then.'

'Go on what?'

'I dare you to eat one.'

Taron nibbles at the tiny, crunchy blue bobbles on the outside of the sweet and then sucks at the jelly, drawing out the agony as if she's performing a supremely difficult and heroic task. She hands me a pink one and I chew it a few times and then swallow it. They're not too bad, actually.

We open the Wagon Wheels and eat some. They taste slightly metallic, with a gritty texture. The imagery on the packaging is reminiscent of the seventies when it was cool to be a cowboy. Wagon Wheels, large, round and roughly hewn, as you would expect from the name, are misaligned biscuits coated with milk chocolate, sandwiching a marshmallow filling. I'm glad the manufacturer didn't fall into the trap of introducing jam into the product. Whenever I go to the supermarket, I find it impossible to resist the offer of a pack of fifteen individually wrapped Wagon Wheels for the price of twelve. I feel a tremendous empathy for the product. I'd like to meet the women in the factory who make the things. I feel as strongly about Jaffa Cakes. We eat them next. I like the elegant mix of dark chocolate and gelatinous marmalade, but also I eat them because the Jaffa Cake is the Robin Hood of the snack world, outwitting the tax man by using a potential product defect—the not-crisp base—to fight in the courts against classification as a biscuit, avoiding VAT and triumphing on behalf of the Jaffa Cake–buying public.

'Jeff and I read in the papers the other day about a rare eating disorder. The sufferer becomes obsessed by fine foods following damage to the front of the brain,' I tell Taron.

'We're safe, then,' she replies, unwrapping another Wagon Wheel.

As we get closer to Weymouth we drive through villages with thatched houses, past farms with homemade signs advertising duck eggs or honey or manure for sale. We smile and read the signs to each other. There are unmanned roadside stalls selling strawberries on an honour system, where you leave the money in a box. 'What happens if you don't pay?' asks Taron.

'I don't know.'

We rumble behind tractors on narrow roads as straw-haired youths with Walkmans, kings of the road, lead a Pied Piper trail of saloon cars and caravans between dual carriageways. Taron and I don't care about slowing our pace. We're on holiday. It's Hi Gloss again: 'You'll Never Know.'

Have we only brought one CD with us?

We're surprised to find ourselves suddenly enter a military zone. Two huge tanks with cannons are coming towards us, driven by youths wearing DJ earphones to protect their ears. The only time I've seen scenes like this is in the publicity shots from the eighties when Mrs. Thatcher was allowed to drive a tank in a field. A camouflaged lorry is behind us, catching up fast. Mild panic seizes me. Is the danger bigger than I realized? Has the British army been sent after us? The lorry overtakes us; the tanks pass by on the other side of the road. We're safe.

'All the land around here belongs to the army,' I remember, wanting to appear calm and rational in front of Taron, who is waving out of the window at the soldiers as if we're spectators at a pageant. 'There are so many unexploded shells near the firing ranges that you can't walk anywhere and it's been turned into a nature reserve.'

'The military turning over the countryside to the wildlife. Cool.'

'Well, not really. It sounds like post-rationalization to me. They stole the land and used it to practice for World War III, and now they're saying it's OK to keep it because of the animals.'

'I wonder what animals they've got.'

'I don't know. I thought for a moment that those soldiers were after us.' My voice is shaky with the absurd confession but Taron is unfazed.

'You're just stressed out. It's good we're getting away. I drove with a girlfriend once from Key West to Miami with half an ounce of coke in the car and we were stopped three times by the police for speeding. We were completely bombed because it's real cocaine in America, not baby powder and laxatives like you get over here. We bought an ounce because we thought it was the smallest unit you could buy in America, not like here where you can get grammes because we've gone metric. An ounce is about twenty-five grammes, and we used up most of our spending money. You can get grammes, of course. If we hadn't been so concerned about trying to look like we knew the score we could have found that out.

'We danced until morning in some dodgy club, and because we'd bought more coke than we wanted it became this enormous problem in our minds. We only had three days left in America, which means we'd have to have taken seven grammes a day to get rid of it. We were carrying so much we kept worrying that the police would think we were dealers if they stopped us. The fear of being stopped began to press on us so much that we bundled straight into the car from the club and drove back to Miami and into the worst storm in years. The sky was black and the rain was so heavy that we only had twenty feet visibility. The other girl was driving, and she kept herself going with espresso and more hits of coke. She'd hidden most of it in a panel in the car, and she wouldn't tell me where so I couldn't incriminate myself if we were arrested. Then we began to think that the police were following us. My friend was so wired she drove as if the devil were behind us and we were stopped and fined three times for speeding. Every time we were stopped they must have radioed on to the next traffic cop over the next border. I thought we'd never get home.'

'Do you think you *were* being followed?'

'No.'

'I had a friend once who took three purple ohms—have you ever had one?'

'No.'

'They're acid, but you could dance on them. He took three of them and was so off his head that he had to get out of the club he was in. He took a taxi, directing it on a wild goose chase, 'right here, left there', that eventually got them back to his house. He could see so many bright lights that he thought he was being followed by a police helicopter and he thought he was on *News at Ten.*'

'What were the lights?'

'Nothing. Just headlights, lampposts. He was off his head.'

When we get to Weymouth we decide to check into the grandest hotel in town, which is on the seafront and isn't very grand at all. I leave Taron watching MTV so I can go and take a look at the place Project Brown Dog is so suspicious about. There's no point involving her as she's not political at all and has no interest in current affairs. She thought a spin doctor was a new name for a club DJ and the allusion was all about 'spinning the wheels of steel' until I put her right.

'Have you got the map?' I ask. 'Or is it in the car?'

'Do you mean the road map or the mental map?'

'What's a mental map?'

'It's like a wish list, but it's an actual picture of something you want to happen.'

'I mean the road map.'

'It's in the car. Do you want to see my mental map?'

'I don't know.'

The mental map is like a primary school art project. She has made a collage by gluing a photo of herself, a photo of me and a picture of a baby cut from a magazine onto an A4 sheet of paper. We're floating together in a disembodied group, superimposed on a view of Weymouth's seaside taken from a tourist leaflet.

'Is this like those Athena Starwoman spells? I've seen one of her books, and every spell begins, 'First take a bath, or a shower.' I thought it was maybe a tricky way of getting teenage girls to wash more often.'

'This isn't magic, it's just using the power of the mind. You visualize something and make it happen. If you believe, you're halfway to making it real.'

I go to the car, consult the road map then drive away from the coast for about five or six miles, heading for the buildings that used to house scientists making weapons to be used with nuclear submarines. The roads are crazy in this part of the country. There's a roundabout every couple of miles, as if the road planners aren't happy at the prospect of anyone getting from A to B in a straight line ('none of your fancy London ways round here'). I reach my destination, dizzily, at the third roundabout.

There are no streetlights, the roads are deserted. I doubt the buildings have been abandoned; they're still very well protected. The offices, laboratories and what appears to be a block of stables on the land are surrounded by fences at least ten feet tall, with spirals of barbed wire on top of them. There is no way I can breach even such low-tech security.

I'm resigned to making an inconclusive report suggesting that although the security indicates the buildings are still in use, I can offer no evidence about who's using them or why. Then my eye is caught by a faint glow at a ground-floor window in one of the office blocks. I take out my night-sight telescope and peer very hard into the window.

I can see a man naked from the waist down, his penis hanging like a long thin worm from his body. A woman moves into view and tugs at it with her mouth, like a chick hungry for a meal. It is my first sight of our enemy, Bird. I take the opportunity to photograph the only feature of his that strikes me as being birdlike, or having any connection to birds, which of course is his penis. The woman with him is his client, Miss Lester, director of services at Emphglott. It's a relief that Mrs. Fitzgerald runs our agency along traditional lines, accepting only money in payment of fees.

16

The Gypsy & The Club

WE GO FOR a walk along the beach before breakfast. The sea is grey. So is the sky. So is Taron, groggy and miserable because she's up so early. Taron collects pebbles and smooth pieces of glass she finds on the beach.

'Why are you collecting the glass?' I ask.

'It's glass in our world but in the shadow world it corresponds to diamonds.'

'Right.'

Weymouth without the sunshine is depressing. The town echoes as we make our way through it back to the hotel. Flags hang from the lamp posts; unlit fairy lights string along the promenade past the clock tower. The town is decked out like a party before anyone arrives, in that sensitive hour when you wonder whether anyone will turn up. We wander past the delivery entrance of Marks & Spencer, the narrow souvenir shops with jaunty striped awnings selling ice creams and shells. The smell of fresh bread is arresting as we pass a baker's shop—the smell the only thing that seems alive in the town. We drift to a halt and peer in the window at the nutty brown loaves, the bloomers, the split tins, cobs and cream cakes. Not a ciabatta in sight. The loaf smell makes me feel a yearning; if only we could attach the smell to Jeff's advert, we would hit all the senses except touch. As we turn away and make for the hotel, I feel desolate and out of place. It's a feeling like homesickness.

We don't really have a plan for the day. I don't feel like doing anything. I'm tired after the drive yesterday and snooping on Bird. After breakfast I go to my room and call Jeff.

'How are you getting on with the advert?'

'I'm giving up on it. We watch adverts on TV, Ali, and we critique them but we never buy the products. I'm not sure if advertising works.'

'Well, what else, then? Why don't you try inventing carton flaps that work?'

'Contrary to what people believe, there's no call for a new design of carton flaps, or at any rate no money in it and no glory in reinventing something. You need to invent something people didn't know they needed. The only way to be sure of hitting the mark is to invent something useless, like virtual pets. You have to invent the need for it at the same time as you invent the product.'

'Isn't that the point of advertising—making people think they need a product they don't need?'

'Yes, I suppose so, but in that case it would have to be product-specific, so I'd still have to abandon the idea of making one ad for lots of products.'

'So what's next?'

'I'd like to create a clock that measures time in the same way people do. So it would speed up for boring things like school or work but give you long weekends and stretch the moments between sleeping and waking so you can have longer in bed. A biorhythmic clock.'

'But wouldn't everyone be on different times? Wouldn't it be really confusing?'

'Yes. You'd have to have a credit and debit account since people would want to gain and lose time in different ways so that you couldn't cheat the system. Maybe it would be better to gain time by finding a way of translating the experience of moving west. Capturing the nature of westness.'

'Like travelling on a plane?'

'Yes. But is it the physical journey that matters? To all intents and purposes you just sit in the same place without moving, although of course the aeroplane is moving. The most important thing is that when you get to the new place you agree with the local people that x equals local time.'

'So maybe it isn't important to translate the experience of travelling west or east?'

'Maybe the important issue is the concept of local time. If two or more people agree on the time then that is the time. Local human time couldn't vary too greatly from real time, and we'd have to use the sun as a guide, of course. Luckily the elliptical nature of the sun's course around the earth means that we accept variations between the winter and the summer performance of the sun. It would be fairly easy for people to grasp the concept of local human time.'

I wonder if Jeff is stoned. He once said he gets a lot of his inspiration when he's done drugs. I've got to hand it to him, most people's approach to time management is to suggest people make lists and be more organized. His is more creative.

I'm still thinking about Jeff when Mrs. Fitzgerald calls me. 'Do you know where your mobile phone is?' she asks me.

'Taron's got it. Hers was stolen in The Raid.'

'No, she hasn't. A man's just called me to say he's picked it up on the sand.'

Taron had the phone with her in her bag. It must have fallen as we walked on the beach, the thud as it hit the sand too soft to be within our range of hearing. The man used the first number stored on my phone and got connected to Mrs. Fitzgerald. He gave her his address and we'll have to visit him to collect the phone before we start looking for babies. I don't tell Mrs. Fitzgerald about my visit to the Project Brown Dog premises because I want to wait until I have something significant to report. I know Bird is involved in some way but there's no point in me telling Mrs. Fitzgerald that; she's the one who told me about it in the first place.

I ring Taron in her room and tell her about the phone. 'I can't think how it happened,' I say. 'Perhaps someone came up behind us and sprayed us with gas, like a Batman villain, and removed the phone from you as we stood frozen on the beach. There's no other explanation.'

'Oh, Alison. Don't be mean. He could be a good contact.'

'A contact?'

'Or he might fancy you. Perhaps it's fate. He could end up being your boyfriend.'

'What?'

'He might make a nice boyfriend for you.' There's no point pretending you don't hear what she's said when Taron is being disagreeable, because she just repeats it for you more clearly.

As it turns out, he's a posh, grey-haired, married man with children who lives in a house that used to belong to George III's mistress, connected by a once-secret tunnel to the hotel in town where the king used to stay. The man and

I don't fancy each other, although he's keen to tell us about the tunnel before returning my phone. He's flattered by our interest in the tunnel ('How romantic,' we coo) and offers us a Welsh cake from a Tupperware container. The Welsh cakes are dry, flat little scones with fruit in them. I take one but Taron smiles coyly at him in the smug 'No, I couldn't' way thin people do when they have just been troughing hotel porridge with prunes.

We take the car and drive to the maternity hospital, which is in a quiet road off the seafront. We don't really talk about what we're doing here, but I suppose we hope that someone will walk through the hospital swing doors with a baby they don't want anymore and hand it to us through the car window.

Taron puts The Chimes' 'I Still Haven't Found What I'm Looking For' on the CD player but I ignore the provocation.

'I like pregnant women,' says Taron as we watch them come and go. 'They're so rounded but they're really vulnerable. Look how slowly they're walking, as if they're worried about falling over.'

Some of them press on the lower part of their belly, as if they're holding the baby in. 'It must be heavy,' I say. 'It must be uncomfortable going around like that all day.' The women don't look serene, but they all have a similar brave expression on their faces. There aren't many men around. Those that do come along look like the proverbial spare prick at the wedding.

I take out my list of recently abandoned babies:

Baby girl found in holdall outside newsagent, 5.30 a.m., Edmonton
6-month-old baby girl in derelict garden, Plumstead

Baby girl found in duffel bag in hospital, East London
3-day-old baby boy in box near King's College hospital
Baby abandoned in Bedfordshire—father found through DNA testing, mother unknown
Baby girl found in alley in South London in supermarket bag
Newborn boy found in bin in Heathrow airport
Year-old baby girl abandoned at University of Hertfordshire
Newborn boy in ladies' toilet in Henley-in-Arden, Warwickshire
Newborn boy dropped into Thames, found near Battersea Bridge
Newborn boy abandoned in woods in Corby, Northamptonshire
Baby boy abandoned near golf course in Bridgend

The baby in the Thames is the only one that wasn't alive when it was found.

'I don't think "abandoned" really covers it,' Taron says. 'It's not as if the mothers leave them to die. It's better than keeping them and neglecting them. They leave them somewhere they'll be found. They want to save them.'

'There is another word. People used to call them foundlings, didn't they? That's better.'

'Yes, it's better.'

We get bored watching the hospital. The pier is just over the road so we wander over to it to get some lunch. As we walk, we leave pennies on low walls we pass so that anyone low down or bent over like children, old people and disabled people will find them and collect them for luck. Taron's got me involved in her long-term programme to improve the world.

'Why are people so horrible to their children?' Taron asks me suddenly.

'I don't know.'

'I was on the pier in Brighton once and this woman was pushing her child along in a stroller. There's a path you can walk on, made of planks of wood laid lengthways over the wooden floor, but they were walking next to it where you can see the sea in the gaps in the floor. The child was looking down and screaming in terror because it could see the sea beneath it. The woman just kept saying, "Shut up." "Shut up, shut up."'

'I know.'

'Why couldn't she have just walked on the path, or told the child that she was safe and they wouldn't fall in the sea? She just kept saying, "Shut up."'

'I don't know.'

We get some chips from a café on the pier with tables covered in blue and white plastic-coated wipe-clean tablecloths. It reminds me of a story I can tell her to lighten the mood.

'I was in a place like this years ago with a friend who was a feminist, who supported the miners' strike and said all men were rapists, who scattered curses in her conversation and lectured, who drew attention to herself and said, "Let them look." I used the sugar shaker instead of the salt and accidentally coated my chips in sugar. My friend made me eat the sugary chips because she was ashamed that I'd been unable to tell the difference between the salt and the sugar. She didn't want me to order another portion of chips in case the people in the café thought I was middle class and lacking in credibility.'

Taron barely glances at me as we eat our chips. Her thoughts are with the frightened child in Brighton.

As we amble back along the pier in a subdued mood, we pass a gypsy caravan with a fortune-telling sign outside. Taron catches my hand and makes me follow her inside.

We sit, buttock to buttock, on a stool in front of a pleasant-looking woman with longish blonde hair and smoker's teeth.

'Is it both of you, then?' she asks. 'That's extra.'

'We're looking for something,' says Taron. 'We need to know if we'll find it. We need to know where to look.'

I take out a notebook and pencil. 'Are you with the press?' she asks sharply.

'No.' I'm secretly flattered. I'd always wanted to be a journalist because I was good at English at school, but the teachers said I wasn't pushy enough. I sometimes feel I should have stood my ground, as I would have enjoyed the lifestyle. However, to appease the gypsy I spend the rest of the interview with my hands gripped together in my lap as if posing demurely for a school photo.

'You're very spiritual,' she says to Taron. 'Take some time every day, visualize what you want, you'll make it happen. You have the power.'

The interior of the caravan is small and cosy, decorated as you would expect with lacy curtains and some knick-knack painted granny flowery things. There are pictures of her with celebrities who have taken time out from playing the summer season or pantomime in the local theatre to consult her.

'Will we find what we're looking for here?' Taron is asking.

'Yes.'

'Really?' I'm surprised by such a direct answer.

'You have a lot of anger,' she tells me. 'You use it as a screen. Be careful, you'll drive away the people you love.'

To Taron she says, 'The sea will restore what you have lost.'

Taron is very impressed and sort of skips all the way back to the hotel, but I'm not impressed. I've never really thought of myself as an angry person, but I'm acting all angry now that she's mentioned it. The thing that's making me cross is that, although I don't believe in her claptrap, I would have liked to ask her about the government buildings, just to see what she'd say.

Our work is done for the day and we decide to have some fun. When we consider our options this means eating something, going to the pictures or going to a bar. 'Did you bring any drugs?' asks Taron, in a gasp of horror as if she's forgotten to switch the bath water off.

I have not brought any drugs so Taron tips her handbag out on my bed and pats everything carefully to see if she can harvest any drugs from the fur and screwed-up bits of paper it contains. She finds an E in a piece of silver paper that she waves at me with joy without looking up, and a few strands of spliff and tobacco mixed with fluff that she discards as being unusable.

'Maybe we can score some spliff from the soldiers. The army always has drugs,' she says hopefully.

'And what would we say to the man on the gate?'

'No, I don't mean we should go to the army base. Just look out for people with short hair in town and see if we can score off someone in a bar tonight.'

My definition of a bar would be somewhere you can sit down, where women are welcome and where you can buy soft drinks and coffee as well as alcohol. Weymouth only has pubs. We tread squeamishly on the richly patterned carpets, ducking under nets and those round, coloured bowl things that are something to do with lobsters and that have been tacked to the ceiling. We inspect the ice bucket on the bar and see that there are only two pieces floating in a lot of water.

'Two Stoli and cranberry, please,' announces Taron loudly.

'We've only got Vladivar on the optic,' admits the barman, whom I note with alarm has short hair. 'Do you want vodka and orange, vodka and tonic, vodka and grapefruit?' We settle for two halves of lager before she can get pally enough to enquire about the local drugs scene.

'Cranberry juice is very good for cystitis, it's a wonder they don't have it,' muses Taron.

'I don't think this is the kind of place where they care if it burns when women piss,' I tell her.

The signs are that we should call it a night and save our London appetites for London, but Taron is on a mission to find some spliff. Seemingly this means we should get wasted first. 'Go on,' she says, holding a chip of white tablet out to me.

'No.'

'Go on, it's only a half.'

'No.'

'Go on.'

We wash it down with the lager and leave. We don't expect much from the local clubs but we're pleasantly surprised.

There are no queues outside the clubs in Weymouth. I hate waiting outside. Even when you're on the guest list you usually have to wait for a few moments while someone checks it. I suppose I've waited to get into a club in summer when it's warm and not quite dark, but I can only ever remember waiting when it's freezing cold in winter, listening to the music coming from inside the club and watching the lasers sweeping the sky through an open door. It's like queuing to get into the future. Huge black men guard the doors wearing jackets that look like expensive anoraks but are probably called something different. The people queuing are runts. Their physical stature has been affected by too much queuing, too many fags, too many Es. Their teeth are chattering and they've already taken the drugs they believe they need to make them dance. It's great never to walk into a club straight. The angles look strange, it's a long way from one side of the club to the other, the music sounds good, everyone is dancing. In Weymouth we don't have to queue and we're not straight when we go in, so we're already doing something right.

The other thing I hate about clubs is when they have too few girls' toilets. Two girls are always skinning up in one of them, talking bollocks. One girl is puking in another, and the rest of us are queuing for the last one. The dance floors are full of glamorous, half-naked dancing princesses but the harsh lighting in the queues for the toilets transforms them into very pale, sweating scarecrows with straggly hair, dilated pupils. Most of them are jiggling, either because they need the loo and they remember that jiggling helped when they were little girls on long car trips or because the drugs they have taken to make them dance can't discriminate between the flaky-paint interior of a toilet and the rammed, pulsating dance floor.

There are no queues for the toilets in the club in Weymouth because no one else is in the club. We automatically check them out anyway. That's all you have to know when you're in a club—exit, toilets, meeting point. Taron finds us a table. 'If we get split up, we'll meet here,' she says, and then we laugh forever because it's absurd. When you're off your head you take very great care of each other. You tell each other when you're going to the toilet and remind each other to drink plenty of water when the heat takes over, or the drugs. It's curiously comforting, a reminder of being a child with a mild fever. Your mum is coming up the stairs with a drink of warm Ribena and life is in a kind of limbo because there will be no school tomorrow.

We go to the bar. 'Let's get pissed,' says Taron. This is a good idea because the drugs are coming up really strong and alcohol will take the edge off the rush. I look over at her and she's chewing gum very rapidly with her head thrown back, like a wild pony. I cling to the edge of the bar and breathe very deeply. I can feel sweat in the creases of my palms and a light tingling at the back of my neck and the top of my right arm as if someone's brushing my skin very gently with a feather. I swipe at my arm in case it's not the drugs and there's an insect there, crawling on my skin. There's a list of cocktails at the bar but I don't think I can tolerate tonight's special 'Malimoo', which is Malibu and milk. I would puke. I'd like vodka and cranberry and grapefruit, strong and pure and clean tasting to temper the rushing and fluttering caused by the drugs. 'Two Sea Breezes and two bottles of water,' I say urgently and sort of snog the drinks with pleasure when the barman finds the ingredients to satisfy us.

It's pub chucking-out time and the club is filling up. We whirl and wiggle to a collection of hits from the seventies, eighties and nineties that I haven't heard since I went to a wedding reception. The playlist includes:

Diana Ross, 'Chain Reaction'
The Weather Girls, 'It's Raining Men'
Abba, 'Dancing Queen'
Wham! 'Club Tropicana'

It's great fun. Our hands are in the air, bottles of water held aloft like sacred chalices as we dance. The atmosphere reminds me of Gay Pride. From time to time Taron and I hug each other, clinging on. 'Love you,' she says. 'Love you,' I say.

We drink loads and loads. Every time I drink, I piss, so I make friends with the girls in the toilets as I'm in there so often. Taron, beautiful and glamorous, dancing to Kylie Minogue's 'Better the Devil You Know', is a magnet for the men. The world is our oyster and Weymouth is the pearl, for as long as the drink and drugs are in our system.

I imagine us finding a baby and managing to keep it. It's as if the baby is with us now and we're dancing to celebrate.

I wake up with a swollen tongue and dry mouth, needing a piss. I have pissed a whole ocean tonight. I'm lying on the very, very edge of my bed because there is someone else in it. Taron lies like a starfish under my covers as she sleeps, her eyes like soft bruises under the closed lids. There is a humming noise in my head, like the noise a fridge makes. Why is Taron sleeping in my bed? If I got off with her last night, I'd like to be able to remember it, at least. I'm wearing my bra and pants and my body bears no memory of sexual experience. I go to the bathroom and look in the mirror. I look great. One of the gifts I have been given by the gods is that no matter how outrageously I spend my time overnight, my makeup will still be intact the next morning. I have a piss and brush my teeth and my tongue; then I go back to bed. I turn Taron over on to her side with her back to me so I can cuddle her like a doll as I go back to sleep.

17

The Runes

BIRD'S MEN HAVE achieved a breakthrough. They have cracked the code used in the address book they still believe belongs to Alison. The implications are so alarming, so important, that Bird calls a summit meeting with his some-time associate, Flower.

'I passed you some names, the other day. Thought you might find them of interest. Did you turn up anything?'

'No, not really. I thought they were a bit of a waste of time.' Bird, a Cambridge man, is not surprised. Flower does not have a very keen intellect. Even so, Bird is so tied up with the work for Emphglott that he will have to rely on Flower for some backup.

'We've cracked a code they use that links them to the criminal destruction in the Republic of Ireland and else-where. Take a look at this.'

Bird takes a piece of paper on which a number of crude code symbols have been solemnly replicated.

'These symbols are runes. Most of them match the symbols used to identify genetic test sites around the world. The *g* symbol appears often but we can't match it to anything at the moment. I'm having someone hack into the immigration computer system to check how many of these people have been abroad recently. I expect it will tell us they have visited the sites to carry out acts of sabotage. This isn't the list of target sites I've been looking for, but it's just as important. It shows the extent of Alison Temple's involvement with these people. I think they're eco-warriors.'

Flower has only the vaguest idea of what an eco-warrior might be, although he watched Swampy on TV on *Have I Got News for You.* He peers pleasantly at the page and taps other symbols there. 'What about these ones?'

♈ ♉ ♊ ♋ ♌ ♍ ♎ ♏ ♐ ♑ ♒ ♓

They're signs of the zodiac. We don't know their significance in this case. I've called off all searches of these people's property and I'd like you to do the same. I don't want to proceed further until we know what we're up against. We must go very carefully, very quietly. I believe I can persuade my contact in Fitzgerald's agency to supply us with information. I need you to work with me on this. I can't trust anyone else. We've searched Alison Temple's house once and found nothing of value. She's the key to this. I'd like you to go back and have another look around, talk to the neighbours, talk to the milkman, talk to the postman. Try and find out more about her and what she knows.'

18

The Hangover

THERE'S SOMETHING NICE about rehydrating a hangover, eating plenty of stodgy food and resting. We haven't reached that stage yet when we wake up. We're still at the bickering, foul breath, headache stage. Light sneaks in through a gap in the curtains, and I can see a bag of grass on the dressing table.

'How long do you think we should stay here?' I ask.

'Dunno.'

'Let's give it one more day. I don't think we're going to find a baby. What would we do with it anyway? We wouldn't really give it to your mother, would we?'

Silence.

'We haven't got anything ready for a baby if we found one. We'd need blankets and things and a cot.'

'It's bad luck to have baby things in the house before you have it.'

'I don't think it counts when you're hoping to find one.'

'I had a good time last night.'

'So did I.'

'Let's keep looking, Alison. I really felt last night as if we'd find a baby.'

'So did I. That's because we were off our heads.'

We laugh about the music for a while and how much we danced. Taron managed to score the spliff off the DJ, apparently.

The other thing we have to sort out is what we're going to do about the names from Taron's address book. If they're on a database somewhere we have to erase it.

19

Betrayal

MRS. FITZGERALD WAITS for Alison to call so she can give her the bad news. The world is a fickle, empty place. There is no one to trust in it. Mrs. Fitzgerald remembers the first time she had to break news of a betrayal to Alison, when she was a client. Mrs. Fitzgerald has to help many young women in this way, but it hurts her when her operatives are affected.

'Mrs. Fitzgerald? I need your help. I need to get inside Bird's organization and remove Taron's friends' names from his files. They must be on a computer somewhere. What do you think?'

'I've just had confirmation that someone you trust is working with the other side, Alison. I think the news will surprise you, but perhaps we can use the situation somehow.'

'Who is it?'

'Alison, it's your neighbour. It's Jeff.'

'I don't think so.'

'I'm sorry. I'm afraid it's true. Dick, my client, is absolutely sure. Flower has been paying him.'

'I'll call you back.'

20

Sheep Dip

I FIND THAT I'm very shocked. I think of every lovely thing Jeff has ever said to me, every innocent conversation, and I find a twisted meaning. He's a shadowy agent working with the other side. Then I remember his poetry and his inventions and I know it's a load of nonsense, so I ring him.

'Jeff,' I say, 'how are you?'

'Ali. Did you hear that thousands of Britain's only native freshwater crayfish have been killed in a river near you? The water was full of Cypermethrin. It's used in sheep dip. Half the river's population of crayfish have been wiped out. That's a lot of sheep dip.'

'Jeff, never mind all that now. Have you ever heard of someone called Major Flower?'

'Yes.'

I put the phone down. I can feel something squeezing my heart, and my face crumples as if I'm going to cry. I'll quite enjoy this but before I give in to the emotion I think I'd better clear things up with Jeff.

'Jeff,' I say, phoning him again. 'What have you been doing?'

'With the advert, do you mean?'

'No, no. What have you been doing with Flower? What are you up to?'

'He pays me for information about you.'

'But are you mad? What do you tell him for?'

'I don't particularly ever tell him the truth. I just say, for example, "She's gone to Nottingham," and he gives me ten pounds.'

'But I've never been to Nottingham.'

'Exactly. I told him you'd been to Ireland and he gave me twenty pounds. Perhaps I score more highly if I mention somewhere abroad.'

'You mad fucking, fucking bastard. I don't know who to trust.'

'You can trust me.'

I try a different tack. 'How's the garden?'

'It's fine.'

'You mad fucking bastard.'

'Ali, come home soon.'

I tell Taron about the betrayal thing and she says Jeff isn't mad at all, and if they would pay her twenty pounds she'd tell them all about me.

'That isn't the point. He paints. He writes me poetry. He loves me.'

'I love you, too.'

'Fuck's sake.'

Taron's been reading up on the local attractions in one of those thin tourist office publications that you can pick up in hotels. She wants us to go for a cream tea before we get back to London, which is OK. Then she gets another cranky idea I'm less inclined to fall in with.

'It says here that women who have been trying for a baby without success have found a cure in a village near here called Cerne Abbas.'

'Taron.' Is she taking the piss?

'They climb this hill in the middle of the night because there's what they call "chalk drawing of a man with a disproportionately large club-like penis" carved into the side of the hill. The woman sits on its cock and when she comes down she gets pregnant. Some couples even do it while they're up there on the hill.'

'Ugh,' we say, in unison.

'Taron, this is a fertility thing, it's got nothing to do with finding a baby.'

'It might help. You can get a cream tea round the corner in a place with a wishing well. We could try that, too.'

'No.'

21

Dick's Girlfriend

DICK, DEFENDER OF the world's defenceless, is feeling miserable and trapped. It's possible that giving Mrs. Fitzgerald the news about Alison's neighbour has brought on this mood in him. It's difficult enough finding friends in this world. Dick has fairly simple pleasures but he knows the importance of finding someone to share them. He has a girlfriend who wears a mohair sweater and kohl pencil round her eyes that smudges almost as soon as she turns away from the mirror. They like watching *Rugrats* on TV on Saturday mornings while he does the washing with an eco-friendly powder that doesn't shift the dirt very effectively.

For a long time, Dick didn't tell his parents that he'd stopped believing in Father Christmas. They went to so much trouble leaving sherry next to the chimney, with a plate of dog food for the reindeer, and he could see how disappointed they would be if they had to give up the deception. Having borne this kind of responsibility from an early age, it would be difficult to alter his behaviour, to become reckless. He'd like to go and grow coffee in Central America in a plantation where the workers are not exploited. He'd like to connect with the world in a more meaningful way. If Mrs. Fitzgerald called him to arms and asked him to dig up sugar beet or swarm naked over advertising agency offices, he'd like to think he'd accept the challenge. Perhaps one of the reasons he cherishes his friendship with Mrs. Fitzgerald is because he knows she's a very steady person and she will never call him to arms.

22

The Spiders

CLIVE FITZGERALD IS crouching in a dusty basement with the spiders, trying to get some peace. In some cultures, the spider is seen as a female and revered as a creator. Clive thinks of spiders as females but he doesn't revere them. He dislikes their silence, the way they appear suddenly beside him on spindly legs. He draws his fingers through the strands of intricate webs stretched across corners of the basement he shares with the creatures, breaking them so the spiders spin them anew between his visits.

Clive is honing the skills he'll need for his new scheme to generate additional income. He has decided to become a graphologist, and he advertises for clients in the local paper. It's important that he does this out of sight of his sister. Even in middle age she watches him and judges him. Her interest emasculates him. He was born clever. He was the one the family watched as he performed ably at school, winning the schoolboy war with logarithms and Latin while his sister plodded behind. His parents thought it sufficient that she had a face pretty enough to marry a solicitor. All her life she has continued to plod, inching her way along life's path, learning a little more each day. Now here she is, running a business born out of the research she undertook for her husband's clients. Clive offered to contact him when he died but his sister refused, saying there was no question she had for him in death that she couldn't have asked when he was alive.

Clive was born clever but he lost the advantage along the way. His character is suited to being feted by servile staff in an expensive office, but he has no career so it's out of the question. Instead he's reduced to crouching in a spidery basement, studying the loops and serifs on people's writing.

'My dear young lady,' he writes to a respondent from the local newspaper, 'I'm afraid you cannot trust the person whose writing sample you have sent to me. He is a very complex person who is hiding a secret.' Clive pauses, running out of inspiration. He does not set out to deceive his clients. It is reasonable to assume that each of us has at least one secret. No young lady should trust a man she knows so little that she contacts a stranger for information about his character.

Above him, Clive hears doors slamming. How he hates to work in an environment full of women, they are always slamming doors. Don't they know if you slam doors you risk trapping ghosts between the door and the frame and they won't return? Clive puts down his papers and books and goes to investigate.

23

Hotting Up

BIRD HAS JUST returned from some pretty tough on-site negotiations with Emphglott, reviewing their security procedures and taking a look at the work their scientists are engaged in. They certainly have more at stake than mutant vegetables. The scientists' work is pioneering, but they claim it meets all the standards and guidelines laid down by the ethics committees, more than can be said for the Lester woman. She all but dissolved when he unzipped his trousers and unfurled his manhood. Her behaviour confirmed his view that there's no place for women in the armed forces and explains why they shouldn't be taken seriously in business. Women are at a disadvantage if they have their mouths full at the negotiating table.

Bird is alarmed at the turn of events when he learns, no credit to Flower's enquiries, that Alison is in Weymouth. It appears she might really be on to something, just as the situation has destabilized, with the scientists unable to breed from the beast they've created and the keeper losing sight of the business objectives. With her address book littered with runes identifying desecrated genetic test sites, like badges of battle honours against the names on the pages, it seems that Alison may even be planning to sabotage Emphglott's premises. If that happens, Bird's lucrative contracts for protecting his client will be terminated and his reputation will be in tatters. Investigations on the names from the address book have so far yielded nothing, with most of the activists having ventured no further than Rimini or Ibiza and no proven link with the destruction of the sugar beets in Ireland. Nevertheless, Bird will persevere until he finds the links he's sure exist.

'Flower? Alison Temple is in Weymouth. Things are hotting up for us. You've been talking to the neighbours. Who's the most important person in her life, would you say?'

The most important person in Flower's life is his wife, but Alison doesn't have one so Flower has to think carefully for a few moments before he answers. 'I think it's her neighbour.'

'Hasn't he been supplying us with information about her?'

'Yes, but it doesn't check out. He's been trying to protect her. I think he's in love with her.'

'OK, let me think about this. We can probably use it somehow. I'd like to find a way to make sure Alison loses interest in my client's research.'

Jeff, like Bird, is thinking about Alison, although with more affection. He has watered her garden conscientiously every evening, waiting until the sun is too weak to draw the moisture back out of the earth, until there is too little heat for the droplets of water collected on the plants to intensify it like a magnifying glass and burn the leaves.

Tonight, in an esoteric departure from Alison's instructions for the care of the garden, he bunches hyacinth bulbs in heart shapes in the borders under the apple tree so their fragrant blue flowers will surprise her in December. He scoops little pockets of earth from the lawn and pushes crocus bulbs among the grass. The delicate maroon petals smudged with paler speckles will spell a message that Alison will see from her bedroom window as the bulbs start to push through the ground. He crouches over the task, a brown paper bag of bulbs beside him. I LOVE, he writes with the bulbs, before his floral graffiti is interrupted by Bird's men. *Who do you love?* Alison will wonder, still worrying about the patent office girl when all this is over and winter comes.

Mrs. Fitzgerald maintains a lonely vigil at her desk. She has stopped working briefly, as she does every day, to listen to the news on the radio as she has her lunch. One item in particular catches her attention. A small group of naked protesters has scaled the building of an internationally acclaimed advertising agency in London to draw attention to its campaign for a company involved in growing and selling transgenic vegetables.

As Mrs. Fitzgerald listens to the report, the crispbread and cottage cheese lie half eaten and half forgotten on her plate. She thinks of the protesters, naked and unashamed, standing triumphantly on top of the building. The unadorned beauty of the men, and the women, too, she supposes, as shocking as if Adam and Eve had broken through the thin fabric that separates the innocence of paradise before the fall and the sophisticated world. Mrs. Fitzgerald imagines the bemused expressions of the agency's creative teams, their embroidered braces straining as they stick their heads out of the window and look upwards to see what all the noise and fuss is about. She doesn't know that braces were a 1980s style accessory and advertising people mostly wear plain black T-shirts these days.

Unable to stem the flow of fanciful thoughts, Mrs. Fitzgerald imagines herself and Dick taking their place among the young people in their futile, heroic campaign on the roof. Her face flushes slightly as she pictures herself dizzy on top of the low building, breathing heavily with the effort of climbing. Police sirens sound in the distance, but the protesters are ready to leave quietly. Their work is done. The world's press, flashlights popping, has gathered below them, uncomprehending of their motives but knowing their audacity and the absurdity of the story will make good copy. Mrs. Fitzgerald and Dick, arms locked together, the fingers of their two hands entwined to make one fist raised in triumphant salute, stand shoulder to shoulder with the scruffy, mud-daubed idealists whose causes they have secretly championed for so long.

Mrs. Fitzgerald wrenches her thoughts back to her office, her desk, her ordered, sensible life. Her mouth is dry. She licks her lips and clamps them shut. *No, no, no,* she thinks. *This will never do.* Her battles against such visions leave her tired and feeling old. She walks into the kitchenette to throw away the uneaten portion of her lunch and rinse her plate. The sun shines at such an angle at this time of day that it reflects directly on the water in the sink drainer, making the surrounding white plastic plumbing glow a rich golden colour. It looks as if an angel is lodged in the pipework, its halo sprouting up into the sink.

Bird is rowing Miss Lester on the Thames, his oars dipping silently in the water. It's a dark night but there's plenty of moonlight. Bird is silent, his face set grimly. Miss Lester is keening in a melodramatic way.

Miss Lester finds the scientists she works with so wishy-washy. Like her heroine, Mrs. Thatcher, Miss Lester has a scathing disregard for intellectuals and consequently is unpopular with her staff at work who are hoping she will fail and be dismissed. Miss Lester is an intelligent fool, educated but with no sense. She's attracted to Bird, with his physical strength and manly bearing, and this morning she fled to London in the hope that he would succour her. As far as Bird is concerned, this isn't the deal at all.

It all goes horribly wrong when Bird returns to his riverside London apartment for post-theatre drinks with his wife, who is usually out of town during the week, and a couple of close family friends. Miss Lester has seductively hidden herself in his bedroom wearing a nightdress (at least she's not naked, thank God for small mercies) and he has had to guide her down the fire escape to the wooden rowing boat he moors there and uses occasionally to shuttle between home and offices in secrecy. Excusing himself from the cosy drinks gathering with a story about national security, Bird finds himself rowing the insufficiently clothed Miss Lester to his offices near Waterloo where he can find her temporary accommodation. At this time of night, the only place he can think of to find clothes for her is from the Salvation Army hostel in Vauxhall, which will be embarrassing. A man with his social standing doesn't want to walk into a doss house and beg for spare items of men's clothing. There is no alternative as, with moments to spare before his wife and friends discovered traces of his unsuitable lover, he had to throw the bundle of Miss Lester's clothes out of the bedroom window where they fell into the Thames like a shapeless suicide.

The disgrace appears to have sent Miss Lester mad. She'd like to be thinking of the Lady of Shalott but instead she thinks of Gaffer in *Our Mutual Friend* as she's transported in ignominy along the Thames. The boat passes under the Albert Bridge, its four turrets, with spires on top, just capacious enough for each one to contain a fairy princess, so long as she never lies down but remains standing up or sitting.

The boat arrives at the padlocked, disused Festival Gardens pier at Battersea Park, and Miss Lester stares at the Peace Pagoda as Bird rests for a few minutes. The name of the pier is painted in faded maroon ink, as if the writing were rusty. From far away, the iron structure of the pier looks as if it's made of wood, like breakers in the sea. The water in the Thames is choppy. Miss Lester clings to the pier and vomits discreetly, her salty tears mingling with the hot, peppery liquid spilling into the river.

24

The Giant

TARON IS REALLY KEEN for us to visit the Cerne Abbas giant.
She says we have to try all the different ways of getting luck
and this is one of them. 'If we call out to the Universe, it will
send us what we want,' she says. I wonder if the Universe will
send her some sense if she asks for it. There's no point me
asking for any; I threw it all out the window with the first sip
of strawberry daiquiri when I met up with Taron in Brixton.

I agree to go along on condition that we stick to some
simple rules. As I don't want to get pregnant and neither
does Taron, I insist that we don't actually sit on or near the
chalk penis. The only acceptable course of action is to hover
near it and make a wish to find a baby. It's not that I believe
in this mumbo-jumbo, but on the other hand I don't want
to take any chances.

We wait until after midnight to reduce the chances of
surprising an infertile couple doing it on the hill. We set
off in the chilly summer night with the usual provisions of
sweets and crisps and a torch. We're distracted from our
preparations for a while by instructions printed on the crisp
packets. The manufacturer makes suggestions about social
occasions where we might like to enjoy our crisps—'with
family and friends in front of TV, on a picnic, in the rain, on

a sunny day or just as a Friday night treat.' It seems they're trying to cover all options, as if by excluding something, a crisp eater would fear hidden danger ('What about as a midweek lunchtime snack?' 'If it's not on the packet, it's too risky to try'). We're surprised they don't mention 'as a substitute for proper food' but we forgive them for not mentioning our special set of circumstances tonight, as we feel that a visit to a symbol of fertility to pray to find a baby is an unusual crisp-eating occasion.

When we arrive, the car park is deserted except for a Land Rover hitched to a horsebox. Both appear to be empty. The Cerne Abbas giant is a fairly crudely executed picture. As we climb, we can pick out the image on the hill because it's a moonlit night and the drawing is marked in chalk. To one side of the giant, our eyes are caught by another patch of white.

'What's that?' I ask Taron. 'Does the giant have a dog or something?'

As we get closer, I shine the torch and we see that the patch of white is not a drawing, but what resembles a giant sheep. It's standing immobile, its eyes closed in apparent rapture as a man on a stepladder, his head turned away from us and buried in its soft fleece, makes love to it.

We clutch at each other's hands and scramble back down the hill, embarrassed and shocked by what we have seen. When we reach the car we're breathless and giggly.

'I'm quite prudish about sex so I've never even watched a porn movie, let alone seen someone having sex before,' I tell Taron.

'Well, I've never seen a man doing it with an animal, that's for sure,' says Taron.

My heart is pounding and my hands shaking, but I want to get away from the car park as soon as possible before the man realizes we may have witnessed his coupling with the sheep thing. I drive a little way down the road to the cream tea shop and park there to collect my thoughts. If I try and drive before I've calmed down, we'll have a crash.

'Did you see what I saw?' I ask Taron. 'Do you think we were hallucinating?'

'Maybe.' She starts giggling and we both laugh really hard for ages. Our laughter goes in waves. When we seem about to compose ourselves, we glance slyly at each other and set ourselves off again. My stomach is hurting and Taron seems actually to be gasping for breath. She opens the car door and stands bending over and making wheezing noises.

'Come and look at this,' Taron calls. I start laughing again because I can't think of any sight that she could want me to look at that would be more surprising than the man on the stepladder, and that sets me off once more. I get out of the car and see that she's peering into the tea shop's garden.

'A wishing well,' she says. The tea shop is closed, of course, because it's the middle of the night. We try the garden gate and it isn't locked so we go inside.

'How much are you supposed to throw in?' I ask.

'Well, if you're making a wish for the world, the best coin would be a French one because of what's printed on it—*liberté, egalité, fraternité*. But as we're making a private wish it doesn't matter. Any coin will do.'

'You know that old Christmas carol, "Joy to the World"? If I was making a wish for the world, that's what I'd wish for.'

'Joy to the world? Yeah, that's nice. But any coin will do for now.'

I find us a ten-pence piece each and we flip the coins up into the air so they spin before falling into the water. We're quiet and serious as we make our wish.

When we get back to the hotel we're cold and tired, still stunned by the night's events. Taron throws her arms around me and kisses me goodnight at the door to my room.

'Goodnight, Taron,' I say.

'Baa,' she says, and I close the door and laugh for what seems like half an hour before I go to sleep.

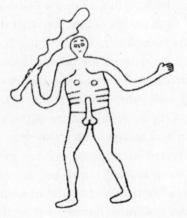

25

Finding Phoebe

'TARON, YOUR MOTHER will freak if we suddenly turn up with a baby, won't she?'

Taron does a very good job of appearing to think about this for the first time. She widens her eyes and tilts her head to one side for ages.

'Let's go and see her and ask for help with destroying the database,' I suggest, 'and then slip in the idea about the baby and see how she feels.'

'The sea is so powerful and magical. Let's park here tonight and meditate and wait for a vision of where we can find a baby. If nothing happens then let's go home tomorrow.'

We park close to the pier and wind the windows down to let the salty smell of the sea into the car. Everything is pink, as if we're trapped in a love bubble. The sand is pink, the sky is pink, there's a track of pink in the sea as the sun sets. Even the boards and the buildings on the pier are painted in pastel colours. A family walks along the beach away from us. The children are skimming pebbles in the water.

'Do you remember there was always tar on the sand when we were children?' I ask Taron. 'Do you think it's still there?'

'I don't know, I always go abroad on holiday.'

The helter-skelter on the pier looks very tall against the skyline. A shining disco ball marks the entrance to the amusement arcade, catching the last of the fading light in the sky. There's a Ferris wheel on the very end of the pier, positioned so you will feel as if you are falling into the water as you go round on it. Tiny pricks of electric light run along the edges of the pier and pick out the attractions but the pier is deserted.

'I'm frightened of the sea,' says Taron.

'I know.'

It gets cold, and we wind the windows back up. We're both very tired. Perhaps it's the sea air; we haven't done much over the last couple of days. Taron smokes a joint, and we start to doze.

The sea is very black. The air is very still. There are almost no ripples on the surface of the water, but I can hear the sea moving and the water washing up on the sand and back again. I stare out at the sea, trying to make out the horizon. I cannot see where the sea ends and the sky begins. The stars are very bright, a shower of electric lights. When I look back at the sea I can see the stars reflected in the water. I didn't notice them before; I only saw the blackness. I can't see where the sky ends and the sea begins. Everywhere there is black and the bright lights and the rushing sound of the water on the sand. At the edge of the water I see something drift onto the sand and lodge there, then dislodge and drift back with the water. It looks like a box or a crate. Or a crib. It's difficult to see because the stars in the blackness are like fireworks and their light distorts everything. I think I see a baby's hand waving from the box, the features of a little moon face turned towards the stars. We have to save it before it drowns. 'Taron,' I shout, 'Taron, wake up.' The words strain soundlessly in my throat as I grab at her. My whole face is screwed up as if I'm crying but the tears are trapped in my throat. We wake up together, clutching and scrabbling at each other.

'Alison,' says Taron. 'Did you see it? Did you see the baby?'

'I think I was dreaming.' I look out at the sea but there is no box, no shower of stars, no mysterious blackness.

'We dreamed the baby. We made it come.'

'But it isn't here, Taron.'

'It's a sign.'

I feel stiff and cramped and disoriented. I think I won't be able to sleep, but Taron and I drift off again into a dreamless sleep.

I wake up very early as the sun is rising, and it looks as though it will be a lovely day, even though a red sky at morning is the shepherd's warning. I shuffle out of the car, hunched over and uncomfortable, and hobble down to the pier to stretch my legs. The sea is a long way out. Low tide. What a strange night. It must have been the dope Taron was smoking with the windows shut. I'll have been high as a kite. My mouth feels very woolly. I'd quite like a cigarette, even though I don't really smoke much, just when I do drugs or I'm drunk. I'd like to go back to the hotel and have a shower and a pee and pack up and go home.

It's then that I see her. Tucked up under the pier near the wall. A baby in a box. Our baby.

I stand there for a while until Taron stalks up behind me. She fishes around under the baby's pink blanket. 'No note,' she says, picking up the box with an effort. 'Let's call her Phoebe.'

We get back to the hotel and put the baby on the bed in my room. Taron winds a strand of my hair round her finger and tugs hard to loosen it from my head. 'We should knot red ribbons in her clothes to protect her. Red for life and knots to confuse the devil. We'll have to use your hair for now as it's reddish,' she tells me.

She slips a key into Phoebe's box, under the blanket, to lock her in this world and stop the fairies from stealing her. I can hardly protest, considering the powerful magic that brought her into the world.

26

The Abduction

MRS. FITZGERALD SITS in her office and waits for Alison to call. Her spectacles are on the desk in front of her and she fiddles with the chain. She has more bad news. On days like this the work gets her down. Mrs. Fitzgerald is fond of Alison. People sometimes say that a younger person they care about is like a son or daughter to them. Mrs. Fitzgerald doesn't feel like this about Alison. A daughter would be a liability, someone to watch every day for signs of the madness that grips her family. She has never wanted children. Alison is just Alison, a good worker, and she's fond of her.

'Alison, I have some bad news about your neighbour, Jeff,' she begins.

'But I've cleared that up. He's not involved with Flower, not really. I told you. He's just been giving him false information.'

'I know. That's the problem, Alison. He's been abducted.' Alison is numb and speechless on the other end of the line. Mrs. Fitzgerald sighs. 'I'll try to locate him and see if we can strike some deal with them, explain his innocence. If we can find a way to free your neighbour, I'll mobilize all the forces I can spare.' She doesn't tell Alison she suspects Jeff is being held by Bird, who is more dangerous than Flower, and who would be menacing Jeff with poisonous snakes if his stash hadn't been stolen by the police.

27

The Disagreement

I WISH SHE wouldn't keep calling him my neighbour. It makes our relationship sound so accidental; it doesn't sound at all as if we've chosen to be friends. It lacks poignancy, too. Would the neighbours of John McCarthy have held a vigil?

I'd been feeling pretty guilty that I hadn't told Mrs. Fitzgerald about photographing Bird and Miss Lester together. It was a kind of betrayal not to even mention the events in Cerne Abbas, which have to be connected to Emphglott because I can't think of anyone else who'd be breeding giant sheep in the area. Now, it feels as if fate might have had a hand in things. If Mrs. Fitzgerald can't tell her client what I know, there can be no possibility of a leak to Bird's organisation and we might be able to save Jeff.

I try my hand at writing a poem for him as I think it's what he would have wanted, under the circumstances.

> *Guardian Angel*
> Jeff, more than neighbour
> My guardian angel
> What's that rustling
> Under your shirt?

Are your wings
Folded there?
Or have you grown hairs on your back
Like the ones on your knuckles?
Like the man turning into a bee
On *Tales of the Unexpected*
When we were children
I love you anyway

I don't send it.

I have to get back to London and sort things out. Part of the reason we came here was to flee the danger in London but now I just want to get home, and bugger the danger. I'll be closer to where things are happening, and I won't feel so powerless. Also, my emotions are in so much turmoil that I feel the way you feel when you're sick and you're like an animal who wants to crawl back to its lair to recover.

Our drive back to London is rather subdued. Taron and I have had a disagreement. We went to Boots to buy baby stuff, and while I was getting vests and bottles and milk formula, Taron shoplifted the nappies. Phoebe is in the back of the car in her box, waving her arms and cooing. Taron has called her mother from a phone box and I'm still waiting for a full debrief. She's taking so long to tell me, I think I can guess what she'll say.

'She doesn't want the baby, does she?'

'She doesn't…she doesn't think a baby can help her at the moment.' We exchange very few words because we're furious with each other, stuck with a stolen baby named after one of Taron's experiments with reality. I grip the steering wheel with an emotion that is close to violence, and when I think about Jeff, it's as if she's to blame for that, too.

I should have been suspicious as soon as she mentioned an apprentice for her mother. As soon as she said the word, all I could see was Mickey Mouse and those stupid fucking dancing brooms in *Fantasia*.

The long drive helps me untangle my feelings. I don't stop feeling angry, but I realize I should be angry with Bird and Flower about Jeff, not with Taron. It isn't Taron's fault that we found Phoebe under such bizarre circumstances. It isn't Taron's fault that Jeff has disappeared. In fact, it's my fault that Taron and her friends have been in danger. By the time we reach Seagram's offices in the Ark near Hammersmith flyover, I have everything in perspective. It helps that Taron doesn't speak at all. She's Anne of a Thousand Days, frivolous and flirty in life but brave on her way to the chopping block.

We stop at the services and attend to Phoebe with a stolen nappy in a cloud of baby powder. The sticky tabs don't work properly if you get powder or grease on them, but Taron and I are wise to this after previous efforts and we improvise with a roll of cellotape. The thought that perhaps they should use Velcro on nappies makes me think of Jeff, and this makes me miserable.

We stop off at my house. The doorstep is covered in milk bottles because he's not there. The house is an empty shell because he's not there. We leave for Taron's place as soon as we can.

Taron cheers up considerably when we get there, skipping around touching her treasures under cover of showing Phoebe her new home. I feel a hundred years old as I make a cup of tea and call Mrs. Fitzgerald. Taron puts a blanket on the floor and plays with Phoebe, yanking off her sellotape-secure nappy so she can wriggle in the nude. They lie with their heads almost touching and gurgle at each other. Taron seems to be a natural with the baby. I have never even touched one before. The closest I have been to a child of this age is looking at a Benetton ad, and that made me feel sick.

I wonder how old Phoebe is. I don't think she's newborn because she's quite pink and filled-out looking, not wrinkly like very tiny babies. On the other hand, she doesn't have any teeth. I consult the baby-care book Taron bought in the service station bookstore and conclude that Phoebe is probably between three and six months. We have weighed her on Taron's bathroom scales by weighing Taron first, then weighing Taron with Phoebe in her arms and subtracting the first number from the second one. Although Taron assures me her German electronic scales are very accurate, I think the results are inconclusive because she appears to be leaning to one side when she's alone on the scales, so I'm sure she's found a way of fixing it so she appears lighter than she is. Can Taron really weigh less than nine stone? Can a baby that small be as much as fourteen pounds?

Phoebe is really very beautiful. I know that all parents are supposed to think their babies are beautiful, but does this rule apply even if you find one and keep it? She has a very fine dusting of blonde hair on her head, as soft as feathers. Her eyes are blue, her feet long and thin, with tiny purple creases in them. We talk a lot about her feet because we see so much of them as she lies on her back and kicks at us. The muscles in her calves are like jelly. The only imperfection is that the tip of her little finger on her right hand is missing from the first joint. I can't think of anything she'd need it for but Taron is ahead of me. 'She won't be able to type,' she says sadly. 'She'll never be able to get a job as a secretary and marry her boss.' I can't be sure whether or not she thinks this is a good thing as I know she has a very romantic view of marriage.

28

Jeff in Captivity

BIRD IS ROWING Jeff along the Thames. Jeff's wrists are bound in front of him with brown sticky tape. He sits in the prow of the boat facing Bird.

Bird rows silently, a loaded pistol resting on the bench between his legs. Looking at Jeff's pale, oval face, long hair and gentle expression, face tilted away from the water, Bird thinks about the painting of the Lady of Shalott in the Tate Gallery.

Dick is eating a yoghurt. When he was a child he thought that yoghurts tasted of sick, and he finds it difficult to shake off the associations now. He eats them because his girlfriend buys them for him and he loves her and doesn't want to hurt her feelings. When he finishes the yoghurt, he telephones Mrs. Fitzgerald.

'Alison's friend is in a secret chamber under the Thames at Vauxhall.'

'Who's got him, MI6?'

'No, the government security forces have got sound-proofed cells in the area but he isn't in one of those. Bird's got him—'

'So it *is* Bird. Do you know where, exactly?'

'Some underground property he uses for interrogation rooms. With that location he's able to mislead people into believing he's connected to the nearby government offices.'

'I know. He's set up his organization in much the same way that people set up language schools and call them Oxford College…I'll have to tell Alison about Jeff.'

'I doubt this is more than a frightener. I think he's taken Jeff as insurance against Alison discovering what Emphglott are doing at their test site. I also suspect Bird has access to information from within your organization, Mrs. Fitzgerald, and that's why he knows where Alison is and why he's so fearful of her.'

'That can't be possible. Alison and I are the only people who know about this project. I've kept Alison informed on a strictly need-to-know basis. She knows nothing about you.'

'I wouldn't worry too much. Information leaks from everywhere. After all, that's why I'm able to tell you what Bird's up to. For your own peace of mind, perhaps you should review who has access to your files. Perhaps there's someone whom you haven't actually told about the project, but who's managed to find out by going through your papers.' Dick tries to handle this carefully. He knows Mrs. Fitzgerald will be upset by the accusation. The motto of her agency is 'discretion assured.' The nasty taste in his mouth is as much due to the unpleasantness caused by upsetting Mrs. Fitzgerald as it is to the flavour of the yoghurt that lingers there.

Bird inspects the sticky tape he pulls off Jeff's wrists before balling it up and throwing it away. Some hairs have come away from the skin. He strikes Jeff very hard on the face with an open hand.

'Now, tell me about Alison Temple.'

In the background the phone rings, insistently.

29

The Rescue

I want to find Jeff and free him. Taron surprises me by coming up with a solution.

'Have you met my friend Derek?'

'No.'

'The one who drums for his masculinity?'

'No.'

'He drums with all these different people. It's a way of getting in touch with your energy. Derek drums for his masculinity but he knows a lot of people who drum for peace.'

'Oh.'

'I used to know him from the clubs. He was a DJ. He told me about the Buddhist monks in Battersea Park. Have you heard the story?'

'No.'

'One hundred Buddhist monks drum for peace under the Peace Pagoda in Battersea Park in shifts, round the clock.'

'I've never seen them.'

'Exactly. They're an urban myth, like the MI6 underground prisons, but I've seen them.'

'Which, the monks or the prisons?'

'I've seen both. You can get to them from the clubs in Vauxhall. Derek and I found them once. Everything's

linked. There are tunnels—disused sewers or maybe something to do with the Tube. It's a maze.'

'Taron.' She's astonishing. 'Let's go tonight.'

I'm very keen to take action. Anything is better than
doing nothing. I ring the agency and ask Creepy Clive to
tell Mrs. Fitzgerald where we're going; then we put on
dark clothes and find a torch. In addition to the torch, we
take pretty much the same things we take when we go anywhere, which is: chewing gum, toilet paper, keys, money,
and cigarettes for Taron. I've stopped smoking since we
found Phoebe. We're going to take her with us as we don't
have a babysitter. We assign her a cover. Taron rings the
club promoter and tells him I'm her girlfriend and we've
adopted a baby and we want to get the adoption blessed
by the monks as we're Buddhist. The promoter tells us the
monks don't exist but agrees to let us into the club anyway,
for old time's sake. Perhaps our matching black outfits—
even Phoebe wears dark colours—convince him that we're
lesbian Buddhists because he wishes us luck as we disappear into a passageway leading from the club's storeroom.

Phoebe is asleep, slung between Taron's breasts in one
of those baby carriers that are supposed to do your back
in if you use them too much. As the door from the club
closes behind us I feel frightened, and I want to turn back.
We're in total darkness and it's quiet. It isn't emptiness I'm
afraid of. Darkness isn't empty for me, it's the opposite of
emptiness. There are layers and layers of the darkness, and
strange patterns of coloured lights give depth and texture
to it. A room can be empty with the light on, but darkness
fills the space, wrapping it up and making a place where the
things you're scared of can hide. I remember to turn on the
torch, and that makes things better.

Taron's friend's club isn't open tonight but others are open nearby. As I adjust to our surroundings, I begin to hear music very faintly and I think I can even feel the vibrations of the bass. We edge forward.

'Which way?' I hiss to Taron. I'm leading because I've got the torch and she's got the baby.

'Just keep going. We turn right eventually. Follow the music,' she says in an ordinary-loudness voice that makes me jump in the quiet.

'Shhh, you'll wake Phoebe,' I say, annoyed. But it isn't that, of course. I hate the way she seems to be taking this in her stride. We creep forward slowly. At first I'm bent over as if I'm afraid I'll hit my head, but gradually I straighten out. The tunnel is quite high, at least ten feet, and maybe six feet wide. It's dry and smells earthy and cold, no worse than a cellar. The torch sweeps over the brickwork as we walk. The music gets louder.

'The music's getting louder,' I say to Taron.

'If we take a wrong turn we'll walk in on an S&M club,' she giggles. 'I think "Leather Sex" is running at the Dungeon tonight.'

We carry on in the same direction but the music starts to fade. 'Not long now,' says Taron. We reach a tunnel dimly lit by electric light. 'Here,' she says, triumphantly, as we see three red doors in front of us.

I try the handle of the first one, very slowly, knowing it's unlikely to be open. Astonishingly, it is. The door opens onto a clean, functional toilet. The second door is locked. The third opens onto a small room. Jeff sits in it alone. He's on a kitchen chair but he isn't tied up. There's a bruise on his cheek and a cut on his lip. He looks very tired. I rush forward and put my hands on his face and then wrap myself round him and squeeze him really hard. 'What have they done to your face?'

'They slapped me.'

I take his hand and pull him after me. I should go first because I've got the torch, but I want to hold on to Jeff so we shuffle about, and I give Taron the torch and let her go first. She's the one who knows the way, anyway.

We walk for about twenty minutes before I realize we're lost. I've been rubbing Jeff's hand in what I hope is a comforting way. 'Are you OK, baby?' I whisper to him.

'Yes,' calls Taron, then stops suddenly so we all bunch up in the tunnel. 'Except that I'm not sure where we are.' She rubs Phoebe's head and I rub Jeff's hand, and we stand there. As usual, I could do with a wee. I should have used that toilet while I had a chance.

'They knew you were coming,' says Jeff.

We press on. We can't hear the music from the clubs anymore but there's another, roaring sound. 'Is that the Thames?' I ask Taron.

'I think it's the monks.'

There's a glow in the tunnels ahead of us. The glow comes from a window. It's more like a serving hatch than a window. It's a hole without glass between this tunnel and another one. We stop and peer through. About twenty monks in saffron robes sit in a circle in a round room lit by candles. They are drumming. The sound is soothing, tidal. They are drumming in a measured, gentle way. There is none of the urgency of men who slap bongos on street corners. You can be fairly sure they are drumming for peace, not for their masculinity. Next time I feel stressed and I want to visualize a calm place, I'll think of this.

We keep walking. There's a room with a huge TV so the monks can spend their time in here watching *Home and Away* between shifts. The room is empty now, presumably because it's very late at night and there's nothing to watch except *Get Stuffed* and the adverts for Chatline 0891 21 21 21. You have to be on drugs to watch that crap. Believe me. The last room is a kitchen. A photograph of a glamorous, very light-skinned Indian woman pinned to the notice board turns out to be Princess Margaret on closer inspection. There are loads of monks sitting around eating Pot Noodles and smoking fags. They don't seem surprised to see us.

'We're lost,' says Taron. A monk with glasses waves at us to follow him and points us in the direction of a staircase.

We climb up and find ourselves back above ground level again in the girls' toilets near the children's zoo in Battersea Park.

'So that's how they get down there,' says Taron. 'I've been round and round that pagoda looking for a way in.' We look over at the pagoda, built of Portland stone and Canadian fir in eleven months in 1985 by a team of monks and nuns from a Buddhist order. The four statues of Buddha facing north, south, east and west and the windbells in the octagonal roof corners are covered in gold leaf. It was the seventieth peace pagoda the order had built, and it was presented to the Greater London Council in 1986. I'm not surprised Taron is so interested in the pagoda. The frantic efforts of the monks and nuns to bring peace to the world by building pagodas all over the place reminds me of Taron's one-woman world-luck-improvement programme.

I cuddle Jeff and rub him all over energetically, as if I'm a midwife and he has just been born. Taron lights a fag and we set off together for home, startling some albino Wallabies who skitter and stare through the fence at us as we pass the zoo. The peacocks hear us coming as we get to the car park and they shriek accusingly, as if we've come to pull out their tail feathers.

I take Jeff home and make him some tea and run him a bath. I'm feeling very guilty. He was abducted because of me. He bore the brunt of the danger Taron and I were running away from. I should have taken him with me to Weymouth.

'They knew you were coming,' he said again. 'They left me in the chair and told me you were coming to find me.'

'They must have had a tip-off.'

'I was all right, I was never in any danger. They just wanted to know whether you knew anything.'

'What did you say?'

'I said it was unlikely because you're not very good at your job.'

'No. You didn't? You don't think I'm bad at my job, do you?'

'No, I just told them that.'

'Who was asking the questions?'

'I don't know. It was a middle-aged man with a big nose and a thin, drawn face.'

'It could have been Bird. I wonder who told him we were coming to rescue you. The only people who knew were Mrs. Fitzgerald and the guy who owns the club.'

Jeff looks very tired. 'You were very brave,' I say. 'Were you frightened?'

'Not really. He kept implying they were working for the government, and I kept thinking, *This is England—they can't do anything to me.*'

'Well, I don't know about that. They're always arresting black people and choking them to death.'

'Thanks, that's reassuring.'

I put lots of foam in the bath and ten drops of an expensive mixture of lavender oil and hops to make him relax. I turn the central heating on and insist he keep the bathroom door open in case he's in shock and slips beneath the foam, loses consciousness and drowns. When he emerges, pink and alive, I steer him into the kitchen to finish his tea while I take a quick shower myself.

He looks vulnerable as he sits and waits for me at the kitchen table, wearing my dressing gown over his grey T-shirt and boxer shorts that I fetched from the airing cupboard in his basement. He stares at the pink rose I've brought in for him from my garden. He told me once that a rose with seven petals was the emblem for alchemists, the forefathers of modern inventors. I removed one of the petals from my rose in the interest of historical accuracy before presenting it to him.

'Don't go,' I say as I step from the bathroom in my pyjamas. 'Stay with me.'

I'll make him sleep with me in my bed and I'll hold him in my arms and cuddle him, like *Babes in the Wood.* The sheets on my bed are fresh and clean because I've been sleeping at Taron's. I light the candles in my bedroom, partly because it will be soothing, but also because I know the fuzzy light is flattering.

His eyes are very dark and he sits obediently on the edge of the bed where I left him, like a child, watching me as I walk around the room putting the match to the candles. I give him a little shove over to the other side of the bed and pull the duvet around us. I'll take care of him to make up for all the times I haven't loved him enough. I prop myself on my left elbow and slip my right arm around his ribs and rest my hand near his shoulder blade. I touch my mouth to his face. 'Baby,' I whisper, as a prelude to stroking his hair.

He rolls me onto my back, pinches my nipple, puts his tongue in my mouth, slides his hand over the silk pyjama fabric between my legs. You know the rest. It wasn't what I had in mind at all. You can have sex with strangers or you can have sex with someone you love, but you should never have sex with your friends. It's too intimate. I know that my face changes when I have sex; it gets softer, my mouth is squashy. I put the heel of my hand against my bottom lip and it is very soft, like a cushion. I try to bite my hand so I won't make the sounds I make when I have sex, but he pulls my hand away. How can I read the newspaper to him and talk about inventions ever again when his body has been inside mine and I have called out his name in my bed? I say his name like a confession. His skin is very soft, his hair is damp at the back of his neck. *Now I know what you look like when you make love*, I think.

'You're lovely,' I say.

'I love you, too,' he says, holding my hand as he falls asleep.

30

Phoebe's Mother

TARON, PHOEBE AND I are lying in Taron's bedroom. Walls painted purple and red are hung with intensively embroidered cloths in threads of gold, orange, red, yellow, indigo, blue and black, stitched by Chinese or Indian hands, sought by Taron in imaginatively stocked shops in Covent Garden and side streets near Tottenham Court Road. Taron, Phoebe and I lie on the Emperor-sized waterbed, Phoebe in the middle, rippling on the gentle waves we make on the thermostatically controlled, non-saline sea that Taron has covered with a patchwork batik bedspread originally from Java. A vase near the bed is crammed with peacock feathers. The hippie womb-fest decor of the room makes me think Taron is over-compensating in case her own reproductive organs have been rendered useless by her lies and excessive use of drugs.

She's breathing very deeply, her eyes closed. Phoebe doesn't stir. We're here to try and conjure up a vision of Phoebe's mother. Taron wants to know Phoebe's real name and what her mother looks like. She claims to have thought of nothing else for a week. In pursuit of the vision of Phoebe's mother, we rock in a watery lullaby on the monstrous bed, floating and bobbing with every slight movement made by one of us. It's starting to get on my nerves.

Then Taron is up and scrabbling about for the half-smoked spliff in the ashtray by the bed. 'I think her mother's about our age, very pale and pretty with brown eyes, and shadows under them where she's tired from crying all the time. She lives in a tower near the seaside, in a lighthouse. Maybe she's tired from staying awake all night to make sure the light's working in the storms, to keep the passing ships from running onto the rocks.'

Taron's grasp of modern radar techniques and even of electricity seems hazy. What does she think illuminates the lighthouse—a stack of non-drip candles from the Conran Shop? Is Phoebe's mother exhaustedly tending a swarm of fireflies imported (like almost everything in Taron's room) from Bali?

'Even though she lives in a tower, she's got short, very dark hair. Her lover has to walk up the stairs when he wants to visit her, as she doesn't have a plait for him to climb. During the day, she lies in her circular room on top of a bed with white embroidered sheets and lacy white pillows. Her bedside table is covered with white coral, conch shells and mother-of-pearl her lover has brought her. She's too tired to get inside the sheets so she lies on top of them and rests—and anyway, the sunlight from the windows all round the room makes it too bright for her to sleep. There are tears on her face. Maybe she's crying because she's given away her baby, or maybe the sunlight is hurting her eyes. She has tiny red lines on her legs where the veins were damaged when she was pregnant, and silver scars on her stomach where the skin stretched. Having the baby made her very tired. She doesn't eat enough fresh fruit because she lives in a tower above the sea and rarely goes out. Her eyes would sparkle

if she had more vitamins, and she wouldn't feel so tired.'
(This is a favourite theme of Taron's.)

'She works too hard keeping the light burning in the
tower. She's only really happy when her lover comes to visit
her. His skin is very dark, and when she kisses him he tastes
salty and smells of the sea. He always brings her a present
when he visits.' (Another favourite theme.) 'She doesn't
know whether his eyes are green or blue because they
change colour with the light. She thinks he's a merman. His
arms are very strong. He pulls himself up the tower's stairs
using the winding metal rail fixed into the wall because his
legs are weak and hurt when he walks. He hasn't come to
see her since she had the baby. She wants to call his name,
she wants to call the baby's name...'

'What name?' I ask, urgently. 'Fuck's sake, what's she
called?'

'I don't know.'

Of course, this is just a story. 'Well, what's his name
then?'

'I don't know, it would be a fish name but I can't think
of any fish names.'

'So, is Phoebe a mermaid?'

'Well, half a mermaid.'

'What's her mother's name?'

'I don't know. A name to suit her elfin features. Elinor. I
don't think she'll live very long. She hasn't recovered from
having the baby. Blood soaks the white sheets when she lies
on them, and every day she removes the sheets and she
washes them in seawater.' Perhaps she, like me, was taught
in home economics at school that cold, salty water is good
for removing bloodstains. I could never see the use for the

information unless you were a mass murderer or a butcher until I realized they were telling us so that we could launder the crotch of our knickers in case of accidental leakage during a particularly heavy period.

'Phoebe's mother washes her sheets in icy seawater and hangs them out to dry on poles sticking out from the windows that go all round the tower in every room. Then she lies down on her bed, freshly made with a spare set of white sheets, and haemorrhages and thinks of her lover and her child.'

'Fucking hell, Taron.' I thought the detail was off the mark, but the distress Phoebe's mother was feeling is likely to be real enough. 'Don't you think we should try and find her and let her know that Phoebe's safe?'

'Well, maybe her mother isn't really dying of a broken heart in a tower. Maybe her father isn't even a merman. It's just, when I think about Phoebe's mother, that's how I think of her.'

Taron conceding that this garbled nonsense may be fantasy?

'Yes, but whoever she is, she's probably missing Phoebe. She's more likely a young girl who was scared to tell her family, but she must wonder if Phoeb's OK. She'll probably spend the rest of her life wondering whatever happened to the baby. She might think she'd been washed out to sea and drowned.'

'We could put an advert somewhere in code so only she would know it was about her baby.'

'What, put an advert in *Bliss* or *Just Seventeen*?— "To the kid who left a baby at the seaside, don't worry, two older women who live together but are not lesbians have taken the child to fight the forces of evil." Or maybe we should ask the sand sculptor at Weymouth to spell out a message on the shore. "We've taken the baby belonging to the merman and the dying woman in the tower. The baby is safe."'

'It's so annoying when you're sarcastic, Alison. Anyway, girls these days don't care whether or not people are lesbians.'

'They do. If they leave a baby to have a better life than they can give them, they imagine the child in the care of a thirty-something woman with a low, soothing voice, smelling of perfume and married to a gentle man with an important job in the City. They don't think of us, stoned and bickering, with wind chimes on our roof terrace.'

'Fuck off.'

'I like the wind chimes.'

'Fuck off.'

'I just think that a disadvantaged teenage mother might not like the wind chimes.'

'Fuck off.'

We sway together reasonably companionably on Taron's waterbed for a while. It feels lovely.

'I want to find Phoebe's mother,' I say. 'And maybe...not tell her about Phoebe in case she tried to take her back, but just...satisfy myself that she's OK. I can't imagine anything worse than feeling regret. She must regret leaving Phoebe without knowing what would happen to her.'

'Phoebe doesn't have a mother, she came from the sea. She only exists because we dreamed her and made her appear. It's magic and you'll spoil it if you analyze it and start looking for a mother. The worst thing for you would be to lose Phoebe, so why do you want to find a mother who will take her away from you? If she had a real mother, she would have told the police by now, and it would be in the papers. She's a magic baby, so just keep the faith and stay cool.'

Now that Jeff is safe, I'm staying here with Taron so we can both look after Phoebe. I'm frightened of seeing him again after our post-rescue sex. Did I inadvertently seduce him when he was in a state of trauma following his abduction? If so, I've probably violated the Geneva Convention. The sex, which was wonderful, changes everything. I blush every time I think of the bruising, searing, beautiful sex and the soft, unprotected words I said to him afterwards. I don't want to go home and face him in case he's one of those people who doesn't respect women that he sleeps with and he casts me aside in favour of the unattainable patent office girl.

I'm not sure if there's still a place for brittle humour in our relationship. Even so, when I read this morning that ten women from a modern sequence dancing club aged between sixty and eighty were rescued by people from a passing steam train as they sank in a peat bog while on a walking holiday in the North Yorkshire moors, I cut out the story and send it to Jeff on a postcard.

I can work from Taron's flat when I have to research stuff on the phone, but I leave the baby with her when I have to go undercover into an office temping—'tempting', Taron calls it, because she says it's tempting fate to do such an awful job and one day I'll wake up and it'll be my real life. She goes out a lot in the evenings, making contacts and polishing up her friendships with people in her address book.

Looking through the book again when we took it out of the bank vault seems to have had a profound effect on her.

I think she thought that life was behind her but when she looked back, she realized how much she enjoyed it. She's talking about getting together a club night and promoting it to make us some money for Phoebe. Quite why this involves going out every night and dancing until dawn, I'm not sure. She's going to call the club night 'Lemon Poppy Seed' because she says that if you eat lemon poppy seed muffins then your urine will test positively for morphine. Quite what this has to do with anything...well, I'm the same age as Taron, but I think I'm getting too old for all this.

I cook for Taron but she's often flitting out and can't stop for a meal, so I'm eating for two at the moment and it's making me thick waisted. Taron's vehement about the need for us to rear Phoebe on unprocessed foods but she rarely has the time to prepare it for her, so I do it.

'Can't stop now,' she yells as my food spits sulpherously on the stove. 'I'm going to check out a new spin doctor.'

Taron's friends rarely come round here but I don't mind too much. If you get a room full of them together, you can see where statisticians get their facts and figures. One in five is gay, one in eight has had a brush with the law, 97 percent are on drugs (the other 3 percent are lying). I don't mind staying in to look after Phoebe, but I feel lonely sometimes. I can't do anything spontaneous, like going to the pictures or meeting up for a drink with friends, and it makes me feel frustrated and powerless. I might just as well be standing at the window watching for my husband again.

It feels as if some of the joy has gone out of my life, but also as if it doesn't matter because what's disappeared is the superficial, selfish kind of happiness that you get from going out or getting drunk and that's been replaced by a greater, deeper feeling of joy because I have Phoebe and I love her very intensely. Aside from decorating Phoebe's cot with garlic, keys and red ribbons to keep her safe from the other world, Taron appears to be losing interest in Phoebe. I let her tie ribbons under Phoebe's cot—not on the bars, in case she gets tangled in them—but I won't let her tie them on Phoebe's clothes anymore because she looks too much like an AIDS fashion statement. I get my way with things like that because I spend so much time with Phoebe. I like looking after her, rocking her till she goes to sleep, watching her sleep, bathing her, playing with her. I never realized before that taking care of someone else makes you love them more than when they take care of you.

I mentioned that a gift I have been given by the gods is that my makeup stays on all night no matter what I get up to. Maybe I should be thanking Boots No. 17 and Maybelline, rather than my sponsors in the heavens. But I have another, more powerful gift, which is the ability to change other people's mood. So if someone is feeling sad I can make them happy. Unfortunately, like any gift from the gods it's difficult to control, so when someone is happy, I try to make them unhappy. This is what's happening with Taron. She doesn't really need me anymore. She's sorted, she's content, she's secure. I spend my time trying to undermine this whenever she comes home. I don't mean to do it but I can't help myself. The other night I came close to sabotaging her four-leaf clover factory. This piece of whimsy is another stage in Taron's plan to beautify and improve the world. It involves leaving four-leaved clovers between the pages of books in WH Smith and Waterstones to cheer up the people who find them. She takes a lot of care selecting the books, and as you would expect, she tends to favour the self-help sections of the bookstores. As it's very difficult and time-consuming to look for four-leaved clovers, she collects ordinary three-leaved clovers, puts them in her flower press, then cannibalizes some of them, sticking on the fourth leaf.

I don't know if she even notices when I'm feeling destructive, as her head is full of her new boyfriend.

When I ask her what he's like she gives me a foxy look and sings the same song, over and over. It's a version of 'My Boyfriend's Back' but she changes the words to reflect the fact that her boyfriend is black and he's Denzel Washington's double.

31

Flower's Wife

FLOWER HAS A very large, light office with a view over the river. Flower's military background has left him with minimalist tastes in furnishings. Unencumbered by obstacles, there is enough room in his office for him to turn several cartwheels if he cares to do so. He doesn't care for gymnastics. Instead, he takes advantage of the space to practice his dance steps. Flower has a dream. He'd like to invent some new dance steps and surprise his wife with them on their anniversary.

Step right, shuffle, turn. Flower's eyes are closed in concentration, his fair hair untidy, his face relaxed and unlined as he retreats inside himself to compose the dance he will dedicate to his wife. He holds his arms out, loosely enclosing the place his wife would take if she were here with him.

The phone rings, interrupting his reverie.

'Flower? It's Bird. Do you have a moment? I need to talk to you about this damn genetic fiasco.'

'Oh yes.'

'Every lead I turn up is a dud. Feels like I'm shooting blanks.'

'What about Alison Temple's friend Jeff? The one I told you about.'

'I asked the boy a few questions but he didn't seem know anything. I was just about to start warming him up when I learned from my source that Alison Temple was on her way to get him. It's just as well, I wanted to use him to get information from her but she has nothing of value. Saved me the job of rowing him back down the river, I suppose.'

'Why are you so sure she has no information?'

'That's why I'm calling you. The names, the symbols. They're a red herring. None of those people have been anywhere near any of the test sites. I've been through all the records at passport control. There's no link. The address book didn't even belong to Alison Temple. She isn't the key to all this.'

'Perhaps it's a bluff? Perhaps it's more elaborate than we think. Who is the key?'

'There is no key. No conspiracy. Fitzgerald's brief was to investigate one of the test sites, not to sabotage the whole bloody lot of them. If it's a question of monitoring the information flow, I can keep track of her reports easily enough through my contact in Fitzgerald's agency. No, there's no conspiracy. We worked out the significance of the zodiac signs.' Bird is spitting with fury. 'Horoscopes. Plain as the nose on your face. Damn silly woman was recording her friends' birthdays.'

Flower thinks of the nose on Bird's face. It's always reminded him of a beak. He imagines Bird's face on the other end of the line, blurred with anger. 'If there's no conspiracy, it means the project is secure. Look at it this way, Bird—it makes our life easier.'

Bird is incensed. Flower always looks on the bright side. Who wants an easy life, anyway, except a lazy arse like

Flower? If he weren't a military man, trained in the control of his emotions, Bird would walk round there now and punch Flower on the nose.

Even if Bird gave in to his baser instincts and went to find him and fight him, Flower wouldn't be there. He's left the office to pick out a spray of his wife's favourite blooms to take home to her. He's blissfully unaware of his part in causing distress to the women and young girls who tend and pick the flowers in Colombia.

Flower, thinking of his wife, is already smiling before he reaches his front door.

'Lilian,' he calls as he pulls his key from the lock and walks into the hallway, not too loudly in case he startles her. 'Lilian.' There's no response. Flower worries sometimes about what would happen to her if he weren't there to take care of her. He left behind the snipers and ambushes that are the hazards of the peacekeeping role played by a modern army and took this job so he'd have the freedom to spend more time with her, and so he could keep a promise he made early in their married life. She told him he looked like an angel when he was asleep and begged him not to let anyone else see him in that unguarded state. It's a difficult promise for a chap to keep on active military service.

Without moving from the hallway, he turns his head and looks through the picture window in the music room and into the garden, in case she's there. There's no sign of her. The garden swing sways slightly on the thick ropes he fixed to the biggest tree last year. The movement could be a sign of interrupted play, or it could be the wind bending the branches.

He tenses, hearing a soft sound nearby. Very carefully, moving only his arm, he sets down the bouquet on the telephone table in the hall and in a smooth, practiced movement he whirls and reaches out in the direction of the sound. The tips of his fingers brush clothing but he's not quick enough. She runs away from him, exploding in giggles at the childish game.

'Lilian,' he calls, laughing. Her shoulder-length unbrushed hair is as blonde as his, bright as a flash of rabbit's tail as she escapes. She wears a loose, shapeless dress, like a child playing in a secret garden in her nightdress. He catches her hand, clasps it strongly, then turns and runs so she can catch him. He's taller and heavier than his wife and it slows him down. Sometimes he comes home to find she's hidden soft obstacles in his way so he'll be easier to catch. She leads him past piles of cashmere sweaters, hoping he'll tangle his feet, or bombards him with feather pillows. She takes care not to trip him with anything that will hurt him.

When they tire of the game, they sit down together and have a drink so they can talk about their day. They never depart from the ritual. She brings crystal glasses on coasters on a little black wooden tray inlaid with mother-of-pearl. Flower mixes the drinks. 'Do you have enough tonic water, Lilian?' he'll say. 'Will you have a slice of lime, my darling?' Always the same questions.

'Did you go in the garden today, Lilian?' He knows how much she loves flowers. Sometimes he worries that she only married him because of his name. Her beauty makes him catch his breath. She looks as young as she did when they married. The only time he's ever seen her cry was on their honeymoon nine years ago, when she saw that he'd put rose petals in their bed. She collected every petal as if he'd spilled them accidentally, and she put them in a dish by the side of their bed.

Flower went to a boys' school. Fair haired, fair skinned, he made a rather good Ophelia in the school play in his final year. Some of the mothers wept at his performance. Perhaps his ability to empathize with women characters, formed during his early years of dramatic training, has helped him to care for Lilian.

Every night he combs and smoothes her hair until it shines like a piece of polished army kit and each strand lies in place next to the other. At night she musses her hair as she moves her head on the pillow with her dreams, and the next day she runs around the house like a scarecrow until he comes home to take care of her again.

32

Phoebe's Ceremony

WE VISIT TARON'S mother in Kent. She's the only person we know who's had a baby whom we can trust with the secret of Phoebe's heritage.

I've stocked up on sweets from Woolworth's for the journey to Kent, but my treasure trove of reminders of our youth has mixed results. Taron's delighted with the Giant Love Hearts, those fizzy sweets in pastel colours that say things like 'Kiss Me' and 'Lover Boy' on them. She's disappointed by the Giant Parma Violets, unfortunately. I love the purple sweets with their delicate, artificial flavour of cheap perfume. It turns out, owing to a miscommunication between us, that Taron was expecting me to pass her a Giant Karma Violet from the packet in my hand. The taste of the sweets can transport you fleetingly back to the seventies but they cannot influence your destiny, hence her disappointment.

I'm not in the least surprised to discover Taron's mother lives in a comfortable semi-detached house, rather than the lighthouse Taron described when she first told me about her. When she lets us in, I catch the warm smell of milky coffee on her breath. She switches off the TV and tucks her feet under her on the sofa as she listens to our story. Taron wants her to name Phoebe or welcome her into the world in some sort of witchy ceremony.

She lights the fire in the grate. 'Warm hearth, warm heart,' she says to me. We unwrap Phoebe until she wears only her vest and nappy and put her on a blanket on the floor. Taron's mother scatters petals around the place as Phoebe gurgles. She loosely ties a tinkling silver bell on each of Phoebe's ankles.

'Let the bells chime with your soul, Phoebe
Child of the world
Child of the sea
Petals bring you beauty from the flowers
Feathers bring you freedom from the birds
Bells bring magic from me,'

she says.

'You work with Ella Fitzgerald, don't you?' she asks me as we're about to leave. I prepare myself for a cheap joke—I've heard a few of them since I started working at the agency. Instead, I get a shock. 'I know her brother, Clive. Be very careful of him. He's a dangerous man. He's a disappointed man. He has no hope, that's what makes him dangerous.'

'Oh him. Taron and I always say he's so creepy that you watch his shadow, as if you might see it move independently. How do you know him?'

'I've come across him trying to get in touch with the spirit world. He wanted to use the power for his own ends. He used to try and use spirit guides for cheap card tricks. He's a traitor, he's evil. I won't have anything to do with him. I suggest you do the same.'

33

The Ace of Clubs

MRS. FITZGERALD SITS alone in the office, her hands over her eyes to stop the tears. She looks like the symbolic representation of someone who sees no evil. It is too late. Mrs. Fitzgerald has seen evidence of evil here, on her own premises. Mrs. Fitzgerald's heart is very heavy. She has been betrayed. She would have liked to talk to Alison but she sees very little of her now she works from home to take care of the baby. She would have liked to call Dick and talk to him, but he might think she was mad. There is nowhere she can turn for comfort. She hasn't even seen the fox for the last few nights as she watched out of her window at home. Perhaps it has lost its struggle with the hazards of modern life.

When Mrs. Fitzgerald sat down at her desk this morning to listen to her voicemail, her foot touched against something on the floor. It was the Ace of Clubs. As she picked it up and turned it over in her hands, its significance was inescapable and brought Mrs. Fitzgerald's own fragile house of cards tumbling down. The playing card was unwelcome evidence that Clive, the king of card tricks, had been sitting here the night before, had probably been sitting here many nights before. It was he who took the call from Alison to say she was going to find her neighbour, Jeff. He and she were the only ones who knew about the mission, and yet Bird knew, too. Clive must have been the one to tip off Bird, her sworn enemy. What other information must he have given them, sifting through her papers, taking her phone calls, whispering with her enemies late at night?

34

Come Fly with Me

THE KEEPER WALKS in the fields with the shig. He's singing very softly to soothe her because she's pregnant. The shig has become more sheep-like and docile since conceiving. The keeper, who has just finished grooming her fleece, has picked a long-stemmed wild flower and tucked it into her fleece near her ear.

The keeper feels very tender towards the shig but he has never been tempted to make love to her again. He did what was necessary for the continuation of the species. Sometimes he even wonders if he dreamed the events on Cerne Abbas hill; the moonlight and the fertility symbol filled him with madness that night. But when he's grooming the shig, the gentle grunting sounds she makes remind him of their secret act of love, and he stands very close to her with his groin pressed against her until his erection subsides. He didn't actually ejaculate inside the creature, of course. Such a union would have been obscene, and his wife would never have understood. At the crucial moment, he withdrew and squirted synthesized shig semen from a turkey baster into his lover's receptive body. Still, he's proud of the part he played in enabling her to get pregnant.

'Come fly with me,' he sings. As he sings to her, the shig grazes among the flowers. With a cracking, booming explosion that can be heard for up to a mile away, their roast-ing pork/lamb and man flesh mingles together for eternity, spraying a final resting place across a very wide area as the shig chews on live ammunition left behind by soldiers who failed their target practice because of their dismal aim.

When the news breaks, Miss Lester begins to clear her desk without being asked, metaphorically bundling her ruined professional reputation with her ruined personal reputation. The death of the shig reflects on the failure of Miss Lester's management style. People are whispering about a suicide pact between the keeper and the shig. Miss Lester will leave it to the professionals to hush up. A couple of weeks ago, Miss Lester wouldn't have believed a word of it. A man in love with a sheep/pig? A sheep/pig in love with a man? But she has been to hell and back in second-hand Salvation Army clothes, and it has made her a wiser person.

35

The Duel

CLIVE, IN THE nation's capital, duels with Taron's mother in Kent. Separated by physical distance, connected by psychic ability, each stands quietly and concentrates on mental combat.

If they were actors in an early episode of *Star Trek* they would be bathed in a greenish aura, the agony of the battle contorting their faces, hands raised to their temples, knees sagging with physical fatigue. The signs of their conflict, though subtle, are there. Energy turns inwards, blood pressure falls, breathing shallows, body temperature lowers. Ashen-faced, chilly, each fights for supremacy. It is a fight Taron's mother has long been preparing for.

Drawing on the strength she needs to protect her only daughter from a servant of the forces of evil, she summons support from around the country from other mothers. Taron's mother sends a stream of images to Clive, forming a rainbow arc across the English countryside; spiders, carefree children with brightly coloured fishing nets, chiming silver bells, assembled characters from the cryptic feel-good tampon ads on TV.

Slowly, slowly, slowly Clive retreats.

36

The Database

TARON AND I have to find a way of removing her friends' names from the database in Bird's organization so they'll be safe. Jeff has been abducted and slapped, Alvin has been kicked. Not one of our friends is safe as long as Bird has evidence of their connection to us. The removal of the names will be our last project together because Taron is so wrapped up in the club promotion. We plan it very carefully.

We wait for the Sunday evening of the August bank holiday so that the office will be deserted. Most invasions and wars are started during weekends or national holidays because the generals and politicians go to their country houses to get pissed and squabble over the barbecue. Drawing from the lessons of history, our attack has been planned and is to be executed with similar logic and military precision, except that we have to bring Phoebe along with us as we can't get a babysitter.

The building we have to break into is a glass-fronted structure near Waterloo that was featured on *Tomorrow's World* in the seventies as the office of the future, with electronically controlled heating and blinds that roll up and down at the windows in response to light from the sun. The reflected clouds that drift across the building's oily blue glass most days are metaphors for the practicalities that cloud all dreams of the future. The blinds at the windows raise and lower infuriatingly as the sun threads in and out behind the clouds. The recycled air in the building is never quite the right temperature for everyone working there and smells of cabbage, even though there is no canteen on the premises. Bird's records clerks are housed cheaply in a suite of offices in the building leased from the council. They moved here from the indignity of the shocking pink Elephant and Castle shopping centre so they rarely complain. I know this because I've been in the building working undercover as a cleaner and I listen to their conversations as I empty the bins and refresh the ladies' toilets. I'm struggling to hold on to the difference between working as a cleaner and being a detective working as a cleaner. At least I don't have to deal with the disposal of sanitary waste; that's a job for the specialists.

We arrive at the building in darkness. Phoebe, seemingly accustomed to these night sorties, dozes between Taron's breasts as usual. We don't actually have to break the door down to get in as I nicked a spare key from the cleaning supervisor. I hate not being able to turn the lights on once we get inside. Taron doesn't seem frightened on our missions, but I am. I tell myself it's OK because fear stimulates my adrenaline and this keeps me alert and sharp, which is what I used to say to myself when I took exams at school, to little effect.

Shadows distort the interior as we walk past the sleeping computers and empty chairs until we reach the place we're looking for. The computer terminal is protected by a password, but the young man who uses it conveniently keeps a note of it on his desk near his Dilbert calendar, along with the passwords of his colleagues. If only he were so meticulous about not throwing his yogurt pots into the paper-only recycling bin.

I log on to the computer. 'This is very important, Taron,' I say momentously. 'We have the future of all these people in our hands. I hope I can do what it takes.' I start scrolling through the names and addresses on the screen. Mine is there, so is Taron's, so are her friends'. We're in a file entitled 'high risk'. There are lots of categories: 'homos', 'nuisances', 'terrorists', etc.

Taron is frowning. 'This is one of the most important things we'll ever do, isn't it? Only I've just thought of something.'

'What?'

'Something my mother gave me. The spell. She said when the time came I'd know when to use it.'

'What?'

'D E L star dot star.'

'What?'

'Try typing it in. D E L star dot star.'

So I type, and all the files start to disappear. I switch off the machine and switch it on again, type in the password. No files. Nothing. We have saved the world, or our bit of it.

37

The Records Clerk

THE YOUNG RECORD CLERK comes into work on Tuesday a little hungover from the bank holiday excesses. Something has wiped all the files from his machine. Perhaps it's a virus, like the Friday 13th virus, except that it's activated by a bank holiday. It seems unlikely, which is a pity as it would have been something to talk about in the pub.

Checking his reflection in the lifeless screen of the computer terminal, the records clerk tries to assess whether the weekend's growth of goatee beard suits him. Possibly not. He strokes the scratchy skin reflectively as he calls the systems people to ask them to get him a new machine. They'll have to pull all the backed-up files from the mainframe computer and download them onto the new terminal, which will be time consuming.

On the plus side, it gives him a chance to swap all the names marked with rune symbols from 'high risk' to 'nuisance'. The order came from the top to do it a while ago, but he's been feeling too rough lately to get going on the task. High risks are passed remotely to someone for action, which probably means regular harassment. 'Nuisances' just stay on the database in case anyone ever asks for information about them.

He shouldn't go out and get so wasted when he has to go to work the next morning; someone could get hurt one of these days.

38

You'll Never Know

I'm back at my house now. It's easier for me to look after Phoebe here while Taron's working at the club. It's the end of summer. There are long shadows on the grass in my garden in the afternoons, and the bluish darkness comes sooner each evening. There are blackberries in the hedges when I take Phoebe for a walk and although I'd like to taste them, I don't pick them in case dogs have pissed on them. Soon there will be that metallic smell in the air as the seasons change and people only go into their gardens for bonfires or fireworks, as if summer was never here.

Jeff has moved away, perhaps because I've neglected him, perhaps because he's too embarrassed to see me again. I can't contact him to find out which it is because I don't know where he's living. I've been too paralysed wondering how he's feeling to think about how I feel, but now that it's too late I know I miss him. I'm not sure how long it will be before I get weevils in the porridge but I'm taking the risk that time is still on my side. I can't bear to throw my cereals away, as it would be an admission that he's not coming back.

The psychic postman brought some post for Jeff this morning as I was leaving the house to take Phoebe for a walk.

'I don't know where he is,' I said, taking the letters.

'That's a pity, you'll miss him,' said the postman, tapping the ash from his cigarette. 'It's a lovely day for autumn, isn't it? Have you heard of a park near Bart's Hospital called the Postman's Park? It was bought by an artist at the turn of the century. He made his money with the painting of Hope blindfolded on the top of the world. He put ceramic plaques round the walls of the park dedicated to unsung heroes: people who saved children from fire, rescued foundlings, that sort of thing.' He looked at me very carefully as he mentioned foundlings. 'You should take the nipper there one day while the weather holds. You might find it interesting.'

He handed me a postcard from Jeff with a poem written on it:

Peace

Heart beating like a drum
It doesn't bring me peace
I can't catch the sunlight
On your kitchen floor

Perhaps it means he's gone off to join the monks. If I search the whole world over, I'll never find anyone who loves me as much as he does. I'm not sure when it happened, perhaps it was when I was staying with Taron, but I seem to have made a choice and chosen Phoebe instead of him. Next time Phoebe and I go to pat the statue of the Brown Dog in Battersea Park, I'll have a look out for him.

We often visit the Brown Dog, even though it takes some finding, stuck away from the glamour of the Peace Pagoda and the fountains on a gloomy path near the Old English

Garden. The statue, unveiled in 1985 by the Greater London Council, who seem to have been terribly busy with monuments in the park that year, replaces the original monument to the suffering brown terrier that was erected in 1906.

> 'Men and women of England
> How long shall these things be?'

asks the plaque.

Phoebe is beside me on the bed as I look out into the garden, watching as the light changes and deepens the green of the foliage in the borders. Like all newborn babies, Phoebe came into the world without possessions, and we quickly amassed them for her. Unlike most newborns, by the time she reached us she had a pink blanket and a cardboard box. Taron and I wanted to keep the box to show her her heritage when she grows up, but it's already disintegrating. I reach out my hand so Phoebe can make a fist round one of my fingers. The CD player stirs into life. It's Hi Gloss, 'You'll Never Know.'

Sometimes, when Phoebe and I are alone late in the afternoon like this, a feeling steals up on me that I recognize because I have always feared it. It's a feeling like melancholy, like realizing at last that I'm grown up because I'm accountable for someone else. I have Phoebe but I miss Taron. I miss Jeff. I love him. If I went out into the garden now I could show you the exact shade of green that matches the colour of his eyes.

The feeling is regret.

Acknowledgements

Thanks to Alex Carr, my editor, and the team at Amazon Encore who brought this book to life: Brian Zimmerman, who designed the cover and the interior of the book; Katherine Giles, who wrote the jacket cover and other promotional text; Jessica Smith, who copyedited the book; and Jennifer Williams, who proofread it. Thanks also to Sarah Tomashek and the sales and marketing team who will help to get the book into readers' hands. Thanks, as always, to Caroline Dawnay and everyone at United Agents.

About the Author

Helen Smith is a novelist and playwright and the recipient of an Arts Council of England Award. In addition to *Alison Wonderland,* she is the author of *Being Light, The Miracle Inspector,* and two children's books. Her plays have been produced to critical acclaim in the United Kingdom. She has traveled all over the world, and currently lives in London.